THIS TIME *around*

THIS TIME *around*

JANE SUEN

This Time Around

This book is a work of fiction. Names, characters, places, and incidents are products of the author's imagination or are used fictitiously. Any resemblance to actual persons, living or dead, events, or locales is coincidental.

Jane Suen books are available for order through Ingram Press Catalogues.

www.janesuen.com

Printed in the United States of America

First Printing: July 2022

Library of Congress Control Number: 2022912617

Ebook ISBN: 978-1-951002-19-0

Paperback ISBN: 978-1-951002-21-3

Audiobook ISBN: 978-1-951002-22-0

To D, and the sweet notes in my locker.

1

Katie raised the airplane window shade, gazing at the gray landscape as the plane taxied down the runway. The magic of flying never got old. The takeoff was her favorite part of the flight—hearing the roar of the engines, feeling the thrust and the shake of the aircraft, and the thrill of becoming airborne. It had never ceased to amaze her.

After high school, she got accepted to college and moved to the city, and stayed there after she graduated. She'd jumped at the offer of an entry-level job at a multinational corporation when the recruiter mentioned a myriad of opportunities for growth. But her sister, Mary, had remained in the small town where they grew up when Dad died two years ago, and Momma had been heartbroken.

"What would you like to drink?" The airline hostess stood in the aisle, positioning the beverage cart.

Katie sat up in her seat and released the tray table, pulling it down.

"Just coffee, please." She nodded, giving a grateful smile and hiding a yawn.

Coffee sounded great. She'd rushed to the airport this morning, barely making it in time. Last night, Katie had less than four hours of sleep. She'd worked in a frenzy to finish her report and click the "send" button on her email. Her demanding boss had made a last-minute assignment, adding it to her list of tasks to do before she could leave.

This job had started out as a dream job, and she had high hopes when Alan hired her. He was a wonderful manager, and he was well-liked and respected by everyone—everyone except the conniving "bitch-from-hell" who plotted Alan's downfall to get his position. This bitch-from-hell became the boss-from-hell—her new nickname was BFH—after she took over his job.

Poor Alan never suspected. Sure, some people had their suspicions and passed hints his way, but Alan was so trusting of this woman, who hid behind her façade, stabbing him in the back as she beguiled him with her fake, poisonous smiles. Katie had defended him early on, but when lies piled on lies, it spread. Thus, some people believed the lies that the BFH seeded far and wide, like planting grass. One never knew which roots would take hold. Katie witnessed her underhanded tactics, abuses, and taking credit for other people's good work firsthand.

"Crackers?" The hostess handed over the coffee cup.

"No, thank you," Katie said, pushing away her thoughts to take the coffee, cupping both hands around the warm container.

She sipped the weak coffee for a while and then gulped the rest of her drink quickly, locking the tray table back up as the captain announced the descent from cruising altitude. They would land in about twenty minutes.

Katie had gotten the wedding invitation from her hometown friend, Laurie, weeks ago. She had tossed it on the mantel, meaning to RSVP later. It got buried under the bills and junk mail. Long hours on the job and other things in life took all her time and energy. She'd simply forgotten until two days ago, when she was going through her bills, writing checks, and came across Laurie's invitation. It was too late to mail in the engraved RSVP. The date of the wedding was this coming Saturday. She didn't think she would go. Hadn't planned on it. Didn't have a plus one. But a voice grabbed her and wouldn't let it out of her mind. It was insistent, pushy, telling her not to let the BFH rob her of this wedding. Katie alternated between fury, disappointment, and fear. Finally, she picked up the phone and called her sister. Mary wouldn't take no for an answer. Said she had to come. Besides, she convinced Katie she'd get there faster on the plane than mailing the RSVP.

Had she missed home? The last time she'd been

back was during the holidays, a few months ago. She'd brought her work home then and wasted her precious vacation time meeting the incessant demands of her BFH. She gritted her teeth. This time, it was going to be different. Coming home was a wake-up call.

Family mattered, her mom and sister.

Other people mattered, too. But with time, some had become distant memories. She remembered the invitation to her tenth high school reunion. She had wanted to go back, but the BFH stole it from her—time she'd lost forever and would never get back.

Katie let out a heavy sigh. She fumbled for the seat belt strap and pulled it, inserting the metal tab into the buckle as the "Fasten Your Seat Belt" sign came on.

2

KATIE HAD PACKED LIGHT, ONE BAG. HER CLOTHES STILL hung in the closet in her bedroom the way she left them. Her mom kept her old room much the same way. She didn't need to bring hardly anything.

As she wheeled her one suitcase to the waiting area, she spotted her sister.

"Katie," Mary squealed, running to greet her, beaming a warm, welcoming smile. Her arms opened wide.

Katie rushed into them, burying her face in Mary's shoulder. She closed her eyes and took a deep breath. She had missed her sister. It was almost like old times.

At twenty-nine, Mary was one year older. She was the dependable one. If Mary said she'd be there, Katie could count on her. They'd been close growing up. When Mary got her first job, she was ecstatic. Soon after, she found an apartment about five minutes from her parents' house and moved in. It was small, but bright and airy. Windows overlooked a courtyard. The backyard had enough room to put up clothing lines. Mary hung her clothes to dry outside. She liked the way the clothes smelled like fresh air and sunshine. She loved her little apartment, and she was proud to afford it on her waitress salary.

Mary had taken classes at the community college while she worked. She could take only one course per semester, but she was in no hurry. Eventually, she'd had enough credits to graduate. Katie had flown home for Mary's graduation. She was proud of her older sister. Her parents were, too. It was the last time all of them were together, and they had a group picture taken. Katie kept a framed copy on top of her bedroom dresser.

"How was your trip?"

"Good. I could have used more sleep last night," Katie said, giving in to another yawn. It was unlike her to complain. Yet she felt she had every right. She had given her all to her job. It sucked every bit of her energy. At night, she'd drag herself home with barely enough energy to prepare dinner. The same scene played out every time. Like a rote robot, she'd reach for the frozen dinner in the freezer and pop it in the microwave. By the time she washed up and changed into something comfier, dinner was ready. The tray was more interesting than the food sometimes, as the food tasted as boring as it was nondescript. It was something to stick a fork in and shove into her mouth. The best part? There were no dishes to wash.

To make it easy on herself, she'd rotate the frozen food trays, with the freshest on the bottom. It saved her from checking the expiration date each time; she only had to get the one at the top. Truth be told, she had microwaved food without checking the date when she was too tired to notice and too hungry to care. If it didn't taste funny, she'd eat it.

Her life was orderly. The only thing that changed was the expiration date on each day's meal. Katie sighed, thinking how pathetic it was for her life to be defined by the order of packaged frozen food.

3

KATIE STARED OUT THE CAR WINDOW AT THE FAMILIAR surroundings as Mary drove. She was born and raised here, and it was the only place she called home.

"Momma's at the house," Mary said. "She says to tell you to relax and quit worrying about your job."

Katie scoffed bitterly. Oh yeah, the last time she was home, she'd buried her nose in her work and stayed in her room. Momma had to pull her out to eat and make her take a break. They hardly had time to chat and catch up.

"Not much has changed," Katie said, as they passed the elementary school where she had swung on the monkey bars. She remembered how high it had been and the time she fell. So many memories. As Mary was a year older, they had the same teachers and knew each other's friends and classmates. She'd even had a crush on this kid who was in Mary's class. Brad. Was he still here?

"You remember the hot-dog drive-in?"

"How can I forget?" Katie laughed. "We used to work there. Remember, we had to wear those silly uniforms?" She had cringed and wished she could hide after Friday night games, when the football players and their dates pulled up to the outdoor drive-in stands in their convertibles with the tops down. It was the hangout place in town. Some kids who knew her had teased her about her uniform, the striped top with the bright hot-dog emblems. They weren't mean, though.

As the car cruised down the one street through town, Katie mused, "Main Street looks about the same."

It was spring, Katie's favorite time of the year. The last of the harsh winter was over. The dingy, snow-encrusted streets swept clean by the spring rain. People were strolling and window shopping as new, colorful displays caught their eye. Others sat on the benches enjoying the weather, soaking up the warmth of the sun. A few stores had their doors propped open to let the fresh air in, clearing out the stale air after months of being closed. Katie removed her sweater and let her arm hang out the window, feeling the sun on her bare skin. She closed her eyes and turned her face toward the breeze.

"There's the Rent-A-Formal," Mary said, passing the store. "Oh, that reminds me. You're going to go to the wedding, right?"

"Yes... no, I mean, I hadn't formally said I was going. But you told Momma." Katie shifted in her seat.

"You didn't RSVP to Laurie?"

Katie shook her head.

"You need to call Laurie and let her know you're coming, pronto, since you didn't send in your RSVP."

"Yeah, you're right. Now that I'm here, I'm looking forward to it. I haven't been to a wedding in years."

"I'll take you shopping. You'll need to get a dress and a gift for the wedding," Mary said.

"What are you going to wear?"

"My pink dress, you've seen that."

"Going with Jim?"

Mary nodded. Jim was Mary's long-time boyfriend. They'd been friends since grade school. They'd been dating for years. Even Mom—and Dad, when he was alive—eventually had stopped asking her when they were going to get married. Mary didn't mention it, either—not anymore. She had ambitions of her own, and she wasn't ready to settle down. When she'd brought up her hopes and dreams with Jim, he had old-fashioned ideas and was less than supportive of her aspirations. But Jim was comfortable, stable, and there were no surprises with him.

"What about you?" Mary asked.

"It's a last-minute decision. I don't have a plus one," Katie said, turning from Mary to hide the tremble in her chin. She allowed herself a moment to feel sorry before shaking it off. Katie was going by herself. Not gonna kid herself that a date would magically materialize one day before the wedding. She straightened her drooping shoulders. She would have preferred not to go alone, but this time, she'd have to suck it up.

4

KATIE WATCHED MARY STICK HER FINGER INTO THE rotary dial of the old-fashioned home phone before giving the handset to her.

Katie pressed the receiver to her ear as the call connected. After some pleasantries, she gave her RSVP to Laurie, who was delighted but didn't let her off the hook that easily. She asked if Katie had a plus one. Katie told her she didn't. Laurie said she had just the person for her. Katie paused when she heard who Laurie had in mind, then hemmed and hawed before answering. Finally, she said, "Okay, you're the bride."

Katie sighed as she handed the receiver back to Mary to hang up.

"What was all that about?"

"Laurie had a fit I didn't have a plus one."

Mary knitted her brow. "Oh yeah?"

"She has a thing about everybody pairing up for her wedding."

"Meaning, you're not going?" Mary asked.

"Meaning I agreed to go..."

"Wait, you just said you don't have a plus one."

"Right, I *didn't*. But now I do," Katie said.

"Explain to me, missy."

"Okay, you know Laurie's cousin Chase, the one who was in my class in school?"

"Uh... you mean your *ex*-boyfriend?"

Katie threw her an exasperated look. She didn't like being reminded he was her ex. "Yes, but didn't he move away or something?" Katie asked.

"He went away for a few years, to college and work. But he came back about a year ago."

Katie hadn't seen Chase since their breakup after high school. He was her first love. It'd taken her a long time to get over the hurt. She wasn't staying in town once she had her diploma. She'd worked hard for her grades and had gotten a college scholarship in the city. College was her ticket out of town. Chase had applied to her school but ended up with a scholarship to another college. They'd separated and gone their own ways. She didn't want to maintain a long-distance relationship during college. Her focus was on her studies. It would be hard enough to juggle school and a part-time job. But a relationship? She wasn't ready for it and couldn't deal with a long-distance boyfriend.

They fought. Chase tried so hard and even talked about giving up his scholarship to come to her school. But she wouldn't hear of it and broke off their relationship. It was the last time they'd talked. It'd been almost ten years now, and she hadn't seen him since.

"Laurie told me he's back in town—and she'd put Chase down as my plus one," Katie said.

"And you said—"

"Well, I tried. But I can't say no to the bride, can I?" Katie rolled her eyes. But she couldn't still the fluttering in her heart or hide the flush on her cheeks at the thought of Chase. What was he like now? Would she recognize him? Had he changed? She turned her face away from Mary as her thoughts of Chase turned private—the way his strong arms locked around her, the deep cleft in his chin, his boyish scent, the warmth of his lean fingers clutching her hand as they walked.

5

CHASE WAS SLICING SAUSAGES AND CHOPPING ONIONS and bell peppers on a handmade wooden board while spaghetti sauce was heating in a saucepan. He splashed a stream of olive oil in a frying pan and, with a swipe of his large, sinewy hand, brushed the neatly cut slices and cubes into the sizzling pan.

"Hey, your cell phone is ringing," Timmy said, picking it up and answering.

"Who is it?"

"Laurie." Timmy held the phone in his chubby little hands.

Chase prodded the pieces in the pan with a wooden spoon, flipping the sausages to get them browned and seared on the other side. He was too impatient for it to cook. The onion was already nice and soft. He turned the heat to low and stepped back.

"Give it to me," Chase said, reaching for the phone

while keeping a watchful eye on the sauce simmering on the stove.

Timmy was only six years old, and he was in the first grade. One of the youngest in his class, he was also one of the smartest. Chase had raised Timmy by himself ever since Timmy's father and mother, Chase's brother Kenny and his wife Darlene, had died in a car accident. They had married after high school. The way Kenny told it, they had made love under the sprawling oak tree. His brother had gathered acorns and said he was nuts about her. She had laughed and said he didn't look like a squirrel. Timmy was the spitting image of his father.

Chase took the phone and held it to one ear while he eyed the pot of boiling water. "Hey, Laurie, what ya doing?"

He made small talk while clutching the phone to his left shoulder as he reached for the box of spaghetti.

"Say what?" Chase barked as he released a handful of dry spaghetti into the pot, which made a metallic screech as the dry pasta scratched against the steel container.

Timmy turned at the sharp tone, not used to hearing his usually calm uncle raise his voice.

"Why did you tell Katie I'd be her plus one?" Chase slammed another sheaf of spaghetti in the pot of boiling water, not even flinching as droplets of hot water splashed on his jeans, then dumped the rest of the box's contents in the pot.

It'd been ten years since he'd seen her, and he'd tried his best to forget Katie after what she'd done to him. He wasn't keen on going, but Laurie would've never forgiven her favorite cousin if he didn't go. His excuse had been that he didn't have a date. Laurie was the meddling sort, but he didn't think she'd stoop this low—with the only person he didn't want to see. One day before the wedding, she'd just turned his world upside down.

Cousin or not, Chase resented the way Laurie stuck her nose in his affairs. Just because she was bossy and related by blood didn't mean she had a right to meddle in his life. But she meant well… and it was her wedding. How could he stay mad at Laurie for long? It wasn't her fault. She'd been like his little sister, and they were close, and she knew how to wrap him around her little finger. Yep, some things never changed.

This thing Laurie cooked up about a plus one… that was a different story. Katie. Hmm, had she changed? Had she been avoiding him? Now, thanks to his cousin, he'd be stuck with Katie at the wedding and the reception. Curiosity raised its head. He wondered what she'd be like now. He'd heard bits of news about her over the years, all complimentary—her graduation from college, the new job at the tallest, fanciest building in the city, and the successes she'd achieved in her life. But wait, was the talk all about her professional life? Hold on… if he was her plus one… then it could only mean one thing: She didn't have one—a personal life, that is.

Chase rubbed his jaw. They were supposed to pretend to be each other's plus one. How much did Katie have to say about it? Or was she duped into it, just like Chase was?

6

MOMMA WAS TAKING A NAP WHEN KATIE ARRIVED HOME. She tired easily these days, and her legs didn't move as fast as she wanted. But her mind was as sharp as ever. Mary had reminded her sister on the drive home, "Don't be fooled by how feeble Momma looks. She's a fighter and will use every ounce of strength to do what has to be done."

Katie smiled, fondly remembering the high-energy, feisty woman she'd looked up to all her life, and had feared when Momma didn't hesitate to give her a whooping she deserved. And Momma could always tell if she was telling a fib. Maybe it was the way Katie averted her eyes or the frantic pleading for her father to intervene, knowing he had a soft spot in his heart for her.

She was Daddy's girl, and he'd saved her from a beating more than once. She swallowed; a rush of pain and regret welled up from deep down, where she'd shoved it, where she hid it. Her chin quivered as tears rolled down her cheeks. When he was on his deathbed, she wasn't there to say goodbye. Katie had been her dad's favorite, yet she never came home to see him—even when he asked for her—until it was too late. He had held on to a thin thread of hope, asking for Katie day after day. Even when others knew it was hopeless, he clung to it until the time he drew his last breath. He had waited and held on in this world for as long as he could. In the end, Katie had hurt him and disappointed him again—and denied his dying wish.

Katie had blamed everyone except herself. Everyone. The guilt she carried would be her burden forever.

It was too late for Katie to undo what she did. She wondered how he could have loved her—a selfish, cold-hearted, and ungrateful child. Dad would be in heaven now, knowing she'd come home to see her mother. Knowing she was too late for him.

Katie curled up on her bed and cried. Her room was exactly the way she'd left it, her childish drawings still taped to the walls. Each piece had its history. She'd kept it all—her collection of dolls and her music jewelry box with the twirling pink ballerina on top, filled with cheap costume jewelry that meant so much to her. It was as if she were still the little girl cranking the handle of the music box, watching the dancing ballerina as the music played. She popped the lid open just to hear it again.

Her bed was pink. Looking at it now through

grown-up eyes, the bed cover had faded, the threads of fabric worn thin from countless washes. Her momma had tried to get her a new set, but Katie wouldn't hear of it. She wanted her soft, old sheets and the pink bed cover. It didn't feel like home otherwise. They also painted the walls of her bedroom that color, a dark shade of pink.

Her clothes were still in the drawers and closet. It was all there—the stuffed animals, her collection of dolls, the small bookcase with her favorite books, framed pictures on the wooden chest of drawers, and her secret hiding place, welcoming her back with their familiar presence.

A knock on the door interrupted her thoughts.

"You doing okay? Need help unpacking?" Mary asked.

"I'm almost done." Katie wiped her moistened eyes. She was glad the door was closed. That was a thing they did growing up—respecting each other's privacy and the need to be alone sometimes.

"Momma's in the kitchen, asking about you."

"Be right out." Katie stood up, smoothing the bed cover and pulling it down over the edges. She took one last look at her room before opening the door. The little girl inside of her ached, and yet assured the grown-up girl. "It'll be all right," her younger self said, as if she were a mother speaking to a child.

7

Momma was sitting at the small, round, eat-in kitchen table with Mary. She seemed thinner than Katie remembered. Maybe it was the way she sat scrunched, with her shoulders slightly rounded. Katie leaned over to hug her, feeling her bony frame under the soft fabric of her plain cotton top.

"Momma," she murmured, putting her lips on the weathered cheeks of the woman she had remembered as tall and strong when she was a toddler, tugging at her dress and playing hide and seek between her legs with her sister.

The hand reaching out to hold Katie's arm was small, but the grip was strong.

"I've missed you," her mother said in a firm voice.

"I know, Momma. But I'm here, and I promise I won't be working this time," Katie said, looking into the steely blue eyes of the woman who would hold her to her words.

Momma nodded slowly, as if sealing the agreement.

"Sit and have some hot chocolate," Mary said as she pushed Katie's favorite mug, the one with the kitties, toward her.

Katie moved to her seat, sliding in the worn chair with the frazzled weave on the backside. Momma threw nothing away as long as it was functional, ever since she could remember. They were poor. She wore Mary's hand-me-downs, but she didn't know any better. But things changed the year she had a growth spurt and caught up with Mary. From then on, they both got new clothes for school.

"We're going to go shopping for Katie's new outfit," Mary said. She turned to Momma. "You wouldn't believe what Laurie just did."

"She talked Katie into going to her wedding?" Momma replied.

"Well, it's more like arm-twisting and an order," Katie said.

"She knows how hard you work," Mary chimed in.

Katie laughed. "Oh, she did more than convince me to go. Laurie got me a date for her wedding, a plus one."

"Who? Don't keep me waiting," Momma said.

"You'll never guess." Katie took a breath. "It—it's Chase."

"She hasn't seen him in ten years," Mary interjected, giving a wink.

Katie felt the heat on her cheeks. Chase was her

old boyfriend. They knew that. But they also knew about the breakup right before she went off to college in the city. It'd taken her years to forget him. She had thrust herself into her studies, and later, her work. Seeing him after all these years was going to be awkward.

8

Chase enjoyed getting up early to make Timmy's lunch. They did it together. PB&J with the crunchy peanut butter, a hard-boiled egg, and a piece of fruit, usually a small banana, grapes, or a mandarin orange that was easy to peel. For variety, sometimes they'd switch out the PB&J for celery with peanut butter, and the egg for cheese and crackers. Timmy was a good eater. He'd never been too picky, and he'd even eat most vegetables if they were tasty. The elementary school didn't have a cafeteria. All the kids brought their lunch.

When Chase clamped the lid on the lunchbox, it was a signal for Timmy to finish his breakfast of cereal and milk and take his dirty bowl and spoon to the sink.

"Get your backpack and let's go," Chase said, holding the lunchbox and walking toward the front door.

It was a short walk, less than five minutes from

their house to the corner of the street where the school bus stopped. Sometimes they had a few minutes to wait before the bus came.

When Timmy was a toddler, he'd get excited whenever he saw the yellow school bus. It wasn't long before it was his turn.

Chase watched the boy get on the bus before he turned around and walked home to get his stuff ready for work.

It was a stroke of luck when this job came up. He applied for it immediately, the day they announced it on the company job listings. Good jobs didn't open often in this small town, and almost never to outsiders in the generations of family-owned businesses. Chase had studied accounting and taken economics and finance courses in college. After graduation, he had worked as an accountant for some small businesses before landing a job at a bank. It was a large regional bank with offices spread in cities and towns across the state.

Chase had kept an eye out for openings in his hometown, and when one popped up, he jumped on it, submitting an application the first day they posted it. It was his chance to move back to the town where he and Timmy's father grew up. He wanted to raise the child here, where he could experience what it was like growing up in their small town. As a single parent, a job with banker hours meant Chase could spend time with Timmy after he got home from school. He was the only family Timmy had, and vice versa.

When Chase was a kid, he wanted to be a fireman, like a lot of little boys. They even went on a field trip once to the town's fire station. A fireman took the kids on a tour and let a few adventurous ones take turns sitting in the driver's seat. The big, shiny red truck was nothing like the toy version he had at home.

It all changed when Kenny and his wife died, leaving the care of their only child, a baby, in his hands. Chase barely remembered how he got through those times, grieving and taking care of Timmy. For a few weeks initially, he leaned heavily on friends and a nanny.

Timmy was a well-behaved baby. But sometimes, he'd wake up screaming and crying at night. He was an orphan, and bawling until he was hoarse did nothing to bring his parents back. It was a void that couldn't be filled, not like the hunger and thirst he had experienced in his life. How did you explain to an infant that he'd never see his mother and father again?

Somehow, the two of them went through the grieving together, surviving the dark period where the promise of the sun or living a life beyond the pain seemed unattainable. Chase didn't realize it then, but as the baby thrived and gained weight, so did his love grow. Timmy had a hard time saying Chase, so he started calling him "cheese" instead. When he got older and he could speak in complete sentences, Timmy dropped the word and called him "Dad".

Chase loved this beautiful child and raised him like he was his own.

9

KATIE HAD NEGLECTED HER NAILS, AND A MANICURE WAS long overdue. It was Mary's idea to get their hair done together and to have a mani and pedi before the wedding. "Why don't we take the day and enjoy ourselves?" Mary cajoled.

Katie smiled. When was the last time she'd pampered herself? She really needed this. Besides, it'd be fun, like old times with Mary.

Mary took her smile as consent and was already on the phone making appointments.

She clicked to end the calls. "We've got our first appointment. You ready?"

"Yes, and we could do some shopping this afternoon." Katie kicked up her leg and wiggled her foot. "I could do with a new pair of shoes."

"Let's get your dress and then match the shoes and accessories."

"Are you sure you don't want a new outfit?"

"Yep, I've got mine all planned. It's the pink dress I wore a few years ago, but it still fits." Mary pursed her lips. "But it wouldn't hurt to dress it up with new jewelry."

Katie knew her sister was saving money to buy her first house. She wasn't frivolous when it came to money. Yet she wasn't tight-fisted, either. With family and friends, her generosity showed.

"Let me treat you. It's the least I can do."

Mary brightened up.

By the time the two sisters had finished their hair and nail appointments and had a quick sandwich at the corner cafe, it was already afternoon.

"What style are you looking for?" Mary asked as she watched Katie try on another outfit, this time a dark maroon dress that was too short.

"Something appropriate for a wedding that doesn't make me stand out."

"You don't want to look the part of an old maid."

"Ouch—and look who's saying this," Katie quipped back, wagging her finger.

"You're not getting any younger, and it's clear you've forgotten how to have fun." Mary crossed over to the racks, flipping the dresses until she found a light apricot-pink one. She whipped it out and held it up, standing in front of a mirror, turning from side to side. "See—this is what I mean."

Katie moved toward the mirror, eyeing the outfit. "Hmm... it's beautiful."

Mary extended her arm, holding the dress by the hanger, and pressed it onto her sister's chest. "Try it on."

The cool fabric touched Katie's skin as she draped it over her arm. It glided, caressing her skin, light and delicate, yet with the strength of countless strands of silk.

She trembled with anticipation as she flipped back the curtain to the dressing room.

As soon as she laid her eyes on this dress, Katie wanted it. She quickly got out of her top and jeans, unzipped the dress, and put it on. Pulling the smooth, silky garment over her head, she felt delectably sinful in the elegant fabric.

Was it time to feel desired again? Deep down, was she thinking of Chase? What would he look like now? How would he react when he saw her? Would he be happy? Did he want to be her plus one?

10

Katie stood in front of the mirror and turned, viewing the dress at different angles.

She fell in love with it, and she felt young and beautiful again wearing it. For years, she had suppressed her feelings and denied her personal happiness to pursue a career.

"Is it too late?" she said out loud to herself.

She stared into the full-length mirror. The answer stared back at her. She saw a smile that looked vaguely familiar and a face that looked hopeful again. Like it was when she was eighteen—when life was simple and uncomplicated, and she was in love—before she made adult decisions for which she hadn't thought through the consequences.

A lump seized her throat, and Katie twisted her neck, stepping back from the mirror.

"Are you okay in there?" Mary asked from outside the curtain.

Katie could hide nothing from Mary. She knew her so well.

She cleared her throat before answering. "I'll be right out," she said. She slipped out of her gown, being extra careful with it.

IT WAS one thing to have agreed to go to the wedding, but it was another to have the guts to go with someone she hadn't seen in ten years and had hurt. Katie didn't buy any accessories. She opened the jewelry box in her bedroom. Inside, she had the perfect piece. She picked up her favorite, the delicate ear drops. The ones Chase gave her when they were together—before she broke up with him and left him with a broken heart. She hadn't worn these earrings since then, but she'd lost count of the number of times she'd looked at and caressed them. Somehow, it didn't seem right to wear them for any other occasion. It had to be a special one like this wedding, with Chase as her plus one. She fingered the drops before she inserted and tugged the wires through her earlobes.

The coolness of the earrings against her reddened cheeks felt good. It sent butterflies through her stomach to think about Chase. She remembered the time he'd surprised her with a picnic basket packed with her favorite foods and drinks. They'd found a place in the woods, shaded by tall, majestic branches. He spread the blanket out for them to sit and eat.

Afterward, they rested. She reclined on the soft cloth, her long hair spilling over the edge of the blanket. He'd lain next to her, propped up on his elbow. His free hand caressed her hair, then his thumb stroked her cheek, stopping at her mouth. She had closed her eyes and parted her lips. When he sealed his lips against hers, it was tender, sweet, and lingering. She'd kissed him back, raising her head to meet his, pressing into him. She had signaled her desire, wrapping her arms around Chase. That day was their first time.

There were others. Would Chase remember their quick romp in the back of his truck? The time he parked under the stars and wrapped the large cotton-wool-blend shawl around her, bundling them together in the chilled air of the night?

It seemed so real, like it had just happened, their times together. These last ten years, she had relived them in her mind. She remembered Chase staring deep into her eyes, brimming with tender love, and hugging her tight in a locked embrace, not letting her go. She held the image in her mind, and it stayed there, for when she wanted—no, needed—to pull it out and replay it, over and over. Over the years, though, the need had receded, and the image in her mind had dimmed and lost its luster, gathering dust.

She choked on a bit of spittle slipping down her throat, and coughed.

Katie had hardened her heart. Put distance between the two of them, cutting the tie with one fell swoop of the blade. Wrenching away from his arms, she'd never looked back. She had been so sure of what she wanted... the big city, the one-in-a-million chance to work for *the* young upstart of a company on the rise so fast, even its executives found their heads spinning.

She'd put her life into that job. What little time she had after work, well, it was used to go home, grab the top dinner on the stack in the freezer, pop it in the microwave, and eat. Some days she was so worn out, by the time she ate, her head would be nodding, and she'd jerk to stay awake. Sometimes she'd click on the TV to see what was on. Most nights, she got home too late for the evening news. She'd settle for silly reality shows, filling the slots of previously well-produced dramas. Sometimes she'd leave the TV on and not watch it. Her tired eyes were seeing, but not really focused.

11

CHASE TOOK A LAST LOOK IN THE MIRROR. HE LOOKED terrific dressed in formal attire. A few faint lines had crept up, adding character to the handsome face that stared back. When Timmy came into his life, he devoted his time to him and bonded with his nephew. He had a family now and a job he enjoyed getting up in the morning and going to. At twenty-eight, Chase was at a place where he was happier than he'd ever been with his life and career—except for one thing: a partner for life. He'd shied away from social functions and the inquiring looks he got when he appeared single, without a date.

Laurie had made it clear to Chase she didn't want a singles' table at the wedding. Her request, in lieu of a wedding present, was for him to bring a date. In Chase's case, he had sweated it out, hoping the busy bride would have other things to do than notice his dilemma. He didn't count on the fact that Laurie was super organized and never one to miss details, especially when it came to her favorite cousin. When Katie arrived in town before the wedding, her prayers were answered.

The call from Laurie was unexpected, and her wish for him to have Katie as his plus one turned his life into turmoil.

Chase blanched at the sound of Katie's name. A chilling blast from the past. Her words still stung ten years later. But after all Laurie had done for him, he couldn't turn her down. He didn't want to be the creep who ruined things. Her wedding was the biggest day of her life, and Chase wanted to be a part of it—a perfect day.

Reliving the sting of Katie's rejection felt like reopening a festering, crusted wound. He'd tried many times to close it and, with it, his thoughts of her. That last day, they had gone to their favorite spot and brought a picnic. He'd been saving all his money and had bought a ring for her. Chase couldn't afford a diamond, not even a tiny one, but he spent every penny he had and bought her a ring that came close. The clerk had assured him a cubic zirconia was the next best thing. Chase had wrapped the ring box inside the cotton napkin and waited with jittery nerves for the moment she unfurled it.

Chase had dreamed of this day, and the moment she discovered the ring. He could hear her squeal with joy and see her face beaming as she shouted a "Yes!" to his heartfelt proposal.

Tears brimmed in his eyes. The rejection was cruel and awkwardly done. His tender heart had felt the stab, and it wasn't softened by kind words or a touch. Blunt, sharp, and hurtful, Katie's words echoed in the deep recesses of his mind, where he could not scrub them out, no matter how hard he tried.

12

KATIE LIKED TO ARRIVE EARLY FOR EVERYTHING—especially today. She woke up extra early and made sure she had time to help Momma get ready and get dressed for the wedding. Then Mary and Katie helped each other with their zippers and last-minute touch-ups.

The wedding was at the church—the same church they grew up attending. Katie scanned the people sitting in the two pews in front and thought she recognized a couple of people she'd known from Sunday school. Momma sat in the middle, between the two sisters. Jim, Mary's boyfriend, slid into the pew and sat next to her. As the hour neared and the church filled, Katie resisted the urge to turn around.

Laurie was a radiant bride, walking down the aisle on her father's arm in the beautiful church adorned with flowers and bridal ribbons. Ryan, the proud groom, stood tall and straight as he waited for his bride. It was a lovely wedding that went off without a hitch.

Katie sighed happily, eyes moist. She felt a squeeze and saw her momma's hand on her arm. She quickly glanced down at her lap, self-conscious of her single status, and then across the pew to where Mary sat with Jim.

Turning to Momma, Katie whispered, "I love you."

THE RECEPTION WAS BEING HELD at Laurie's favorite restaurant, where she and Ryan had first met. Ryan had been a year ahead of Laurie in school. She had seen him around, but they hadn't actually spoken to each other. The day they met, Laurie had gone to the restaurant with her family for dinner. It was her birthday, and the family's tradition was to eat out.

It was on a Saturday night, and the place was jam-packed. During the meal, Laurie had accidentally bumped her glass of cola and knocked it over, spilling the drink on the table and floor. She tried to catch the attention of the waitress, but she was busy taking orders from customers at another table. As Laurie bent down to wipe the liquid with her napkin, a pair of brown work shoes entered her line of vision—her first close-up of Ryan was his feet. As the story went, it was love at first sight, literally—as Laurie stood up and they bumped heads, then she locked eyes with the man in the busboy's uniform.

That was then... and now the restaurant had closed off the entrance and put up a sign, "Private Party," on the door for the afternoon reception. Inside, the place was decorated with streamers and strings of sparkling lights. The tables were covered in white tablecloths and pushed toward the sides, leaving a cleared center area for the dance floor. A large rectangular table was reserved for the bride, groom, and bridal party. Fresh flowers adorned each table as floral centerpieces. In a corner of the restaurant, there was a long table for the DJ.

Katie entered the reception, holding her mother's arm and supporting her. Laurie had been understanding and supportive when she'd expressed her desire to accompany her mother and sister while upholding her agreement with Chase. She waved Mary off to look for a table. The room was crowded already as the festivities started, the sounds of talk and laughter and clinking glassware all around them.

"Here we are," Mary said, taking Momma's other arm and leading her toward a quieter area, a table at the side, and pointing to the empty chair beside Momma for Katie to sit.

Katie helped lower her mother in the chair before she sat down beside her. She laid eyes on the centerpiece, the bright, colorful flowers in the crystal vase tied with a bow and ribbon.

"Like it?"

She turned her face toward the masculine voice, staring at the man who'd just taken the seat next to her, and blinked—twice. Her mouth slacked open. It was unmistakably Chase, but as a fully grown man. Suave, impeccably groomed, and so handsome. She struggled to find her voice. "Chase..."

13

CHASE HAD GLIMPSED KATIE IN THE CHURCH, SITTING eight pews in front of him. At first, he wasn't sure, having only seen the back of her hair. But he kept watching—the tilt of her head, her profile as she turned to talk to the woman sitting beside her—and caught a drift of her laughter as it wafted in the church's lofty interior. It had a familiar ring. He knew in his heart it was Katie.

After the ceremony, the wedding guests went to the restaurant for the reception. Chase stayed back, watching Katie and her family enter the restaurant and chat with the newlyweds.

Chase followed, stopping by the head table graced with an eye-catching centerpiece to congratulate the couple. He couldn't resist teasing them about how they'd met in this restaurant when Ryan had taken an extra shift that weekend, and if it hadn't been for that, he wouldn't have been working that Saturday when Laurie came in with her family.

It was Laurie who gave Chase a slight push and gestured to the table where Katie and her family sat. "Go on."

Chase made a funny, exaggerated face and put his palms together in a plea.

"Do I have to?"

She giggled. "My wedding, your date."

He rubbed his palms together, the sweat clinging to his hands.

"It's been... how long?" Laurie asked.

"Ten years."

"You haven't talked to or seen each other since?"

Chase shook his head from side to side. "No."

"Aren't you curious?"

"You know what happened... how we broke up." Chase paced his words. He'd made no attempt to contact Katie all these years, nor had she reached out to him. What he'd once felt for her had cooled. The desire in his heart was for revenge—for breaking his heart.

Laurie wrinkled her brow. "I didn't mean to butt in. I thought I was helping."

"Well, cousin, I'm finally over her. Took me years." Chase tightened his lips as a grim look took over his face.

"I told her you'd be her plus one." Laurie smiled coaxingly. "Don't make a liar out of me."

Chase leaned down to kiss her cheek. “You have my word.”

14

Katie's eyes traveled from the trim haircut to the familiar face she knew so well, from so long ago. She remembered the soft brown eyes and the cleft in his chin she adored. The smile lines had deepened on his cheeks. But something was different. The eyes that met hers today weren't warm and worshiping. She had snuffed out the light in them and wiped out the hope—they were gone now. The dark pools of brown had changed, and glimmers of fury smoldered in their depth. Katie shivered as their eyes met.

"I—I didn't really expect to see you," she mumbled. She had known he was going to be her plus one, but now that Chase was actually here—in flesh and blood and inches from her face—she stuttered, at a loss for words.

"You wouldn't, except I promised Laurie." Chase straightened his back.

There was a moment of awkward silence.

Katie bit back her tongue and the quick lashing at the tip of it. Perhaps it was the disappointment or her wounded pride that made her want to strike back. But she realized she had no right to expect anything different after what she'd said and done. She'd wounded him. It was written all over his face. She read it as her heart sank. But it was too late. The words spoken years ago could not be unspoken, nor could she gather them up and stuff them back into her mouth. In one moment, she had killed the light in his eyes and smashed his heart.

"I—I'm sorry," Katie whispered.

He gritted his teeth.

"I've thought of it. The words I used were hurtful, but I was young and impetuous."

Chase shook his head.

"I've said it many times out loud when I'm alone—and wanted to tell you in person," Katie said.

She'd had plenty of time—ten years—to relive this part, over and over again. The hurt look on his face had burned into her mind. Yet she'd stuck to her guns, refused to take back what she'd said, and left town without a look back at the man whose heart she had broken.

A fork tapping on a glass got the attention of the crowd and quieted them. Toasts were raised to the happy couple. The DJ announced the newlyweds and spun the music to their favorite tune as Laurie and Ryan stepped onto the dance floor for their first dance.

Then the bride danced with her father, joined by the groom's parents and the wedding party.

Katie watched as the wedding guests joined in on the dance floor, her feet tapping on the floor and her body swaying slightly to the music. It'd been too long since she'd had fun, and she was determined to enjoy it, even if it was from the sidelines. She glanced across the room and saw a group of people standing and talking. One of them seemed familiar, but she couldn't place a name with the face. Maybe he felt her stare. The man turned around and spotted Katie. As he broke away from his group and started walking, and it was clear he was heading toward her, Katie cringed.

"Do I know you?" he asked, placing his hand casually on the back of her chair.

Katie blushed. "I don't think so."

He leaned in, peering over her, staring intently before a smile broke.

"Why, if it isn't Katie Simmons."

She scrunched her nose, trying harder to place him. "I think I know you—"

Mary swiveled her head, hearing their conversation. "Brad!" She jumped out of her chair, scratching the floor as she pushed its legs out and startling Katie, who wondered if Mary remembered her crush on him in elementary school.

He laughed, turning into her outstretched arms to hug her.

"When'd you get back?" Mary asked.

"Last night."

"Where are you staying?"

"At the hotel."

Mary put her hands on her hips. "You should have called. Jim's got room at his house."

"No, I'm good." Brad smiled. "It's just for two nights."

"You're leaving tomorrow?" She made an O with her lips.

"Afraid so. I've got a busy schedule at work."

"Well, it sounds like you're doing well," Jim said. He stood up and clapped Brad's back.

They shook hands.

The DJ put on a snappy tune. "C'mon, everyone, I want you all on the dance floor. If I haven't seen you wiggling your booty and shaking your legs, I'm gonna call you out."

Holding the palm of his hand out, Brad whispered in Katie's ear, "Would you like to dance with me?"

She got up from her chair and slipped her hand in his.

15

A sinking sensation gripped Chase. His chest tightened as he watched Katie swirling on the dance floor while the room throbbed with the pounding bass of the speakers. She was laughing, throwing her head back. Brad had asked her, and he had not. He was supposed to be her proper date, a promise to Laurie, he chided himself. Other thoughts pushed back. *She's an adult, no longer eighteen, and she's free to dance with whomever she wants.* Still, something didn't quite sit right, and he couldn't wait for the song to end.

When the music stopped, Katie didn't come back. Brad was saying something to her now, bending his head to her ear, and she laughed, touching his arm, as the two of them stayed on the dance floor. It seemed like an eternity, but it was only a few seconds before the music started again, a slow dance. Brad took her into his arms, and she closed in, putting her face on his chest. Even as Chase growled and willed his butt to stay seated, he couldn't help but notice how they made a striking couple. Brad, perfectly groomed in his expensive formal attire, and Katie, loose hair cascading down her back in her form-fitting silk dress. Chase scowled as Brad's hand moved up and down Katie's back.

But Chase wasn't the only one who noticed. When the notes signaled the song was nearing an end, a blonde woman split from the group Brad had been a part of. She was dressed in smart-looking, pricy, glittering attire, and she effortlessly took over, replacing Katie in the next dance.

Chase shot out of his chair, stunning himself at how fast his body moved before his mind had a chance to think it over and put a halt to it, and rushed to Katie's side. Her mouth dropped open, a blank look on her face.

"May I have the next dance?"

"I—"

"Would love to." Chase finished her sentence and grabbed her hand as the DJ played the next song.

KATIE BARELY RECOVERED her shock before Chase swept her away. Flustered and caught off-guard, she fidgeted in his arms, her hand flailing as she reoriented her body and made sense of this. This side of Chase was new to her and exciting. He exuded a strong masculinity. His cologne paled in comparison.

Ten years ago, Chase was a gangly, awkward teenager. He didn't know how to dance then, and he was all feet and clumsy. But despite it, he'd asked her to the prom. Katie didn't know it at the time, but found out later how elated he was when she said yes, and that he'd asked his Sunday school teacher, the young pastor's wife, to show him some dance steps.

It touched her heart when she found out how hard he'd tried and how determined he'd been to succeed. He'd surprised her on prom night with a beautiful corsage and the sleek limo he'd rented, splitting the cost with friends. She hadn't expected it, but with the sincerity of his heart, the shy, gawky guy had danced his way into hers.

16

Chase glanced down at Katie's face, upturned toward him as they danced under the sparkling disco balls, the lights, and fabric swags draped across the ceiling. He remembered the prom and Katie, his date. They were so young and naïve. He saw her in his future, nothing and no one else. Senior year, the prom was their last hurrah before they became adults and stepped into the real world. It was their last celebration, the biggest event at school.

Would she remember that night? He remembered how she'd looked at him then—her face lit up with a beaming smile and shining eyes. He remembered how they'd clung to each other in the slow dances and his racy pulse and the stirring in his loins.

THEY LOST TRACK OF TIME. The DJ made the announcement that the bride and groom were leaving on their honeymoon. Soon after, the reception started winding down. Chase was wrapped in the moment, caught between his memories of ten years ago and the reality of Katie's warm arms encircling him now as he inhaled the scent of her light floral perfume. He had planned to make an excuse and leave, heading out early. He didn't plan on dancing with her. He didn't order the quickening of his heartbeat when she smiled and laughed at his jokes, and her soft, small fingers nestled in his hand.

He saw Mary approach with Jim, each supporting her momma as she walked.

"We're heading out," Mary said.

Katie raised her head, her hair ruffled. "Time to go?"

The sisters exchanged a glance, and Mary said, "You guys stay. Jim and I will take Momma home."

"I don't know. Are you sure?" Katie hesitated, tilting her head.

"I'll give her a ride home," Chase said.

"Then it's settled," Mary said, smiling. "You know where the spare key is, Katie. Don't wake Momma up when you come in."

After they left, something shifted in the environment. The interruption broke the moment, the dreamy state he'd entered. He took a step back.

"Hungry?" Chase cocked his head. "How about

some caffeine and dessert?" It popped out of his mouth.

"Coffee sounds wonderful, and maybe a slice of cake or pie."

"I know just the place."

CHASE LED THE WAY, pulling out the keys when he reached a shiny red truck.

Katie stopped in mid-stride, gaping at the new vehicle. "This is my ride?"

He grinned and unlocked the passenger door, giving a slight bow. "Your seat is waiting. Step right up."

"Wow, this is a great-looking truck," she said, getting in.

He took her to a diner at the edge of town. It was a new place that opened up about five years ago, sparsely decorated and clean.

They picked a table and slid onto the smooth benches. The tabletop had streaks of wetness, having been just wiped with a damp cloth. The waitress came back with a dry towel and two menus.

"Hi, what can I get you?" She held a pen poised over an order pad.

"Two coffees, please." Chase paused, studying the menu. "And a slice of your homemade pie."

"What kind of pie do you have?" Katie asked.

"We've got apple, peach, and custard pie."

"I'll have the custard," Katie said. "I can't remember the last time I had homemade custard pie."

"Make it two," Chase said, handing the menus to the waitress and noticing the tag pinned on her uniform with her name. "Mabel."

He sat back, arching into the curved bench seat. "The pies are delicious. They make them fresh every day."

"I can't wait to try it," Katie said.

He wondered what had gotten into him. Chase hadn't planned to be in a diner or to have anything to do with Katie. He had fulfilled his agreement with Laurie and should've left hours ago. A mix of emotions churned inside him. He remembered how she'd betrayed him. Cut up his heart and served it up on a platter. He'd held a grudge for ten years. He wondered, had she ever known how he felt or regretted what she'd done? How had her life been since? Was it worth it leaving her hometown and going to the city?

His thoughts were cut short when the waitress came back and brought two mugs of steaming coffee.

"I just made a fresh pot."

The waitress turned around and walked back to the counter, picked up the two plates of pie slices, and returned to their table. "Anything else?"

Chase glanced at Katie, and she shook her head.

"Thank you, Mabel. We're good," Chase said, flashing a smile.

"You kids enjoy."

Mabel walked away, her cushioned heels silent on the tiled floor.

17

THE CREAMY CUSTARD PIE SLID SMOOTHLY DOWN HER throat, its sweetness coating her taste buds. It was every bit as delicious as Katie had imagined and more. She had craved a homemade pie, its wholesome ingredients a welcome change from the boxed grocery store pies she usually bought.

Katie took a tiny sip of her hot coffee, peering at Chase under her lashes. She hid a smile behind her mug as her lips parted, surveying the man sitting across from her—attractive and self-assured.

Chase was no longer the shy, gawky kid she knew ten years ago. This man was an eyeful—handsome and well-groomed. Her eyes took in every inch of his chiseled face, achingly familiar yet distant. She longed to run her fingers through his thick brown locks and touch the special dimple in his cleft chin that she loved.

She gulped, taking another sip. Her tongue flicked

out to catch a drop hanging on the edge of the cup. She licked her lips and set the mug down, relaxing her back on the bench seat.

She hadn't seen Chase for almost a decade. She had wondered about him, although not on purpose, on her infrequent visits home. It made it easier, not running into him when she finally managed to put him out of her thoughts. Yet in the back of her mind, he'd stayed, like a stage actor behind the curtains, waiting until the next scene.

He was so different from the boy she remembered. He exuded masculinity and charm. When he walked, he took firm, confident strides. On the dance floor, Chase easily led her, taking charge.

Katie licked her lips again. He looked delicious in his formal attire—his chest filled his shirt, and his arm muscles bulged, stretching the fabric of the sleeves. She was tempted to reach out and squeeze his arms and feel the rippling muscles underneath. She bit her lip. Chase was all man now—but he wasn't hers.

The shy boy Katie remembered had grown and emerged as an adult. His face was no longer smooth and unlined. It had taken on the years, although they had been kind to him. She felt the ache in her heart, thinking of the time she had missed.

Her fingers toyed with the mug, running down the curve of the handle and around. She'd decided ten years ago. At times, she'd wondered if she'd made the right decision. Over the years, she'd struggled on her own. Katie had kept a strong demeanor at work, but at night, when she was all alone, she'd wept into her pillow. She had missed him. She held on to the good parts of their time together, pushing away the part when they broke up—when *she* broke up with Chase.

It was engraved in her mind—the agony on his face gave away his heartbreak and pain. She did it to him then, delivering the blow. One fell swoop. Katie had reminded herself it was better that way, to be over and done with quickly. She had stood firm, keeping her pride intact.

When Katie left, it didn't feel good. She didn't feel righteous or victorious. She didn't expect—and wasn't prepared—for the pain in her heart. The dull ache inside her throbbed and stayed long after her memories faded.

18

Chase stared at Katie, noticing she was quiet.

"You okay in there?"

She took a deep breath and sighed.

Chase perceived some sadness, but she didn't elaborate and didn't talk about it. He didn't press her. Almost reflexively, he responded by reaching out to grip her small hand, covering it with his. He felt something—was it a spark?

She didn't pull away.

The waitress appeared with a full pot of coffee.

"Refill?"

Chase nodded, retracting his hand. He gestured at Katie and waited as the waitress filled hers. Then he slid his mug toward Mabel, murmuring a "thank you" when she finished.

"Nice wedding," he said, changing the subject when they were alone again. "Laurie worked so hard on it."

"Laurie looked so beautiful, and she and Ryan are so perfect together."

"Yeah, they are."

"And a house with a white picket fence?" Katie teased.

"They rented a small place with a fence. It's cute."

"Did you help them move in?"

Chase grinned. "Sure did. Laurie was thrilled when she found that house. They don't have a lot of furniture yet, but they are so happy."

"Dream come true," Katie murmured, wistfully looking up into space.

"So, how about you?"

"I—I'm okay. Got a good, steady job. Pays the bills and then some."

"Still at the same company since you graduated?"

"Uh, yes. I've worked my way up."

Chase picked up his mug, watching the steam curl and rise. "You know, I just moved back to town about a year ago."

"I think Laurie mentioned it," Katie said.

"Yeah, she's been bugging me for years, but then... this opening at the bank came up, and I went for it."

"You work at the bank?"

"Yup, the one and only bank in town." He grinned sheepishly.

"So you got hired."

Chase nodded. "I came back for the interview with Timmy. Then they offered me the job."

Katie frowned. "Timmy?"

"You heard about my brother Kenny and his wife Darlene?" Chase whispered, fingers white-knuckling his napkin.

"The accident... Mary told me. I'm so, so sorry."

"Their child, Timmy—I'm raising him. I'm his mother and father."

"I can't imagine what you went through."

Chase choked and tried to find the words as a wave of sadness rushed over him. The pain, raw and pulsing, ran through his body. It had never gone away. It had been just the two of them. Kenny was his older brother by a year and a half. They had grown up together—shared the same bedroom. Sure, they had fights and disagreements, but the bond between them was tight. Losing his only sibling created a deep vacuum that could never be filled. His eyes moistened as the memories came flooding back.

Katie touched his hand, offering a tissue.

19

KENNY AND DARLENE HAD BEEN HIGH SCHOOL sweethearts. That's when they actually dated, but they'd met long before, in grade school. Katie had heard about them from Mary, who was in the same grade. Of course, they weren't sweet on each other then, but Darlene had had a crush on Kenny ever since the day he stood up for her on the playground.

A bigger boy, a bully, had pushed Darlene as she climbed on a step to get on the slide, and she fell to the ground. She didn't cry out, but her knee was skinned and bleeding, with fragments of leaves stuck to it.

Kenny was elsewhere on the playground when he heard noises and shouting. He ran over and found Darlene crumpled on the ground, protecting her knee. The bully loomed over Darlene, screaming at her, his spittle flying. Kenny rushed him immediately, tackled the bully to the ground, and punched him in the face, causing his nose to bleed. It'd probably looked worse than it was because of the blood.

By then, a teacher had heard the ruckus and rushed over to see what was the matter. Without a word, she grabbed Kenny's wrist and pulled him off of the bigger kid.

Both boys were dragged off and whisked to the principal's office, and the parents were called. The boys got punishments, but the bully got it much worse. He had to apologize to Darlene.

Darlene went to the nurse's office to get her knees checked out, cleaned, treated, and bandaged. She was lucky it wasn't more serious. She told Mary that Kenny was her knight in shining armor. But he became more than that. He was her first love. And she was his.

They'd married right out of high school. Kenny went to community college and also worked the night shift at the burger joint. Darlene got a job at the grocery store. They were poor, but rich in ways money couldn't buy. They worked and saved every penny they could for their future. Later, when Darlene was seven-and-a-half-months pregnant, she'd quit at Kenny's insistence. He took on another part-time job at the pizza joint.

Money got really tight for them, and Kenny worked every day until he was bone-tired for their little family of two—and the baby on its way.

20

Chase had promised her a ride home. Although he was her plus one, Katie had been adamant about going to the wedding riding in the family car with her momma and her sister. He didn't pick her up. Laurie had mentioned to him that she knew it was Katie's wish since her mother rarely stepped out of the house for a social occasion, and this was important to her.

They left the diner and strolled across the parking lot. Outside, it was a warm, dark night. The sky was hazy. The clouds had drifted, obscuring the moon. A light breeze blew, scattering Katie's hair.

"You know the ridge you took me to on our first date?" She studied his profile and paused. "The spot you picked with the spectacular view on the hillside overlooking the town? I'd like to see it, and the sparkling lights at night."

"Yes, I'll take you." He put the truck in reverse, turned it around, and steered out of the parking lot.

Chase remembered the ridge. He knew exactly the spot she was talking about. Now, as he drove, he couldn't stop thinking. He groaned inside. What right did she have to ask him? What good would it do to relive the past? He remembered sitting in his car, self-conscious of the fact that he was all alone with her. He was shy, tongue-tied, and laughed and made nervous jokes, not sure if she'd think they were funny. Then he tried to get closer, casually flinging his long, scrawny arm on the back of the car seat, resting it a fraction of an inch from her soft, fluffy curls. When he'd plucked up enough courage, he stretched his fingertips, gently playing with and pinching stray strands of her shoulder-length hair. She'd pretended not to like it at first, snatching his hand away—until she didn't let go of him. He thought he was in heaven.

IT'D BEEN AN EMOTIONAL NIGHT, from the intense highs of the wedding to the deep lows of Chase's pain. Katie's heart went out to him, glimpsing the grief that still ripped through him and the responsibility he'd shouldered raising little Timmy. She saw him differently now—a matured man still carrying his anguish and sadness.

Wrapped in her own thoughts and silent during much of the ride to the ridge, an overwhelming sense of loneliness flooded through her. She shivered, even though it was a warm, balmy night.

Chase swung the truck into the parking space on the hillside, the headlights drilling into the darkness. He parked, turned off the ignition, and got out, meeting her on the other side.

The view from the ridge was breathtaking, tiny lights twinkling in the distance, lighting up the town. "It's beautiful," she said, taking in the view, leaning back on the vehicle, bending one knee, and putting her foot on the front bumper.

The wind blew gently on her cheeks. In the distance, faint night sounds provided a soothing background.

"Did you know only male crickets chirp?" Chase asked.

Katie couldn't see his expression, but he seemed more relaxed, calmer.

"No, tell me why."

"I read in a magazine that males will make this sound for mating to attract females."

"Like now?"

"Mostly during daytime."

"This is one of my favorite spots."

"I haven't come up for years. I'm glad you suggested it."

They stayed out there for some time. She didn't know for sure how long, and he hadn't checked his watch. Somehow, it wasn't the same. The first time they were here, it was different. They were open, sharing and giving of their hearts with the innocence of first love. Butterflies had fluttered in her stomach then.

She felt his closeness now; his arm brushing against hers sent ripples through her body. *Katie*, she thought, *get a grip*.

Yet Katie couldn't heed her own words. All she could think of was this strong man beside her, who outgrew the boy he was, and yet remained vulnerable inside. She felt protective. Maybe it was the guilt of having left ten years ago. Or maybe it was knowing how much he'd been hurt, losing his only brother, who left a child to be raised by him, the uncle, since the grandparents were no longer alive. She reached out for his hand.

"Katie..." The anguish in his raspy voice spoke volumes.

She couldn't see his face clearly in the darkness. But she felt his hand pushing hers away.

CHASE DIDN'T WANT to be reminded of his loss and pain tonight. He'd gone to great lengths to push those guilty feelings down, to forget the horrible night when Kenny and Darlene had died on their way to see him. But they never reached their destination. It had happened quickly on the highway. The oncoming car had veered out of its lane into theirs, and the drunk driver had hit his brother's car head-on, killing the couple instantly.

He didn't want to let his guard down in front of Katie again. She was the woman who'd shattered his heart and filled it with more pain again when he saw her tonight. He gritted his teeth.

He hadn't been to this spot for years, and being here brought back those early memories of their first date.

When she grabbed his hand, so large it completely covered hers, and turned around to face him, he hardened his heart and pushed her away.

The clouds had shifted as they floated across the night sky, unveiling the full moon tonight.

He could see her face clearly now, under the soft glow of the moonlight. Her eyes, twin pools of light, focused on him. She stroked his cheek, tracing the outline of his lips, then down to his chin, zeroing in on his cleft. He could smell her perfume, a heady and maddening scent with a trace of lavender entangled in the light floral fragrance.

"We can't—" he growled, as a surge of resentment reared toward this woman who had rejected him and crushed his heart years ago, and a distant voice of warning chimed in.

Before he could finish his sentence, she'd sealed his lips with a melting kiss. He tasted her, felt her soft lips part. His heartbeat quickened as a rush of blood flooded his veins. He wanted it all—revenge *and* this rising desire, urgent and growing, raging through him.

He buried his hand in her thick mass of curls, twisting them to one side. Her eyelids widened at the sight of his flushed face and the heat of his intensity, then fluttered closed as she arched into his deepening kiss.

His vision blurred as his hands roamed her body, exploring slowly.

She'd slipped her fingers down, tracing the V-neck of his shirt to the first button holding it together, tugging it.

In a hoarse whisper, he croaked, "Do you want me?"

She undid his top button in response—then all of them.

He swooped her up, carrying her to the truck. She stretched out on the back seat, waiting for him.

He joined her, stripping off his clothes and undressing her, caressing her smooth body, feeling the softness of her skin. Her arms tightened, pulling him closer. He tasted salt on her skin and inhaled her heady scent. Felt her nails dig into his muscled back. Saw the look on her face. A primal urge took over as his breathing quickened. Consumed by a hunger and thirst of a different kind, he gave in to his desire.

Afterward, he kissed her cheek, felt the wetness. He lifted a strand of damp hair stuck to her skin and tucked it behind her ear. He kissed her again, tenderly.

He thought he heard her say, "I love you," as he nuzzled her ear, and then he whispered it back.

21

A REPEATED KNOCKING AT THE DOOR WOKE KATIE UP. Her hands groped the tangled sheets and pulled them over her shoulders. She blinked, taking a second to get a fix on her surroundings, as her brain confirmed she was in her childhood bedroom. A glance at the clock on the bed stand showed it was nine in the morning. She stretched and yawned.

"Breakfast is ready, sleepyhead."

"I'll be out in just a minute," Katie yelled back to Mary.

Swinging her legs over the bed, she noticed the clothes tossed on the floor. She stood up and quickly gathered her dress, chiding herself and thinking it wasn't like her to be so untidy. Katie sat back down on the bed, fingers caressing the smudged and crumpled dress she wore to Laurie's wedding. Then it all came back to her—last night with Chase. He'd dropped her off at home, and she used the key hidden under the flowerpot to let herself in the house, taking care not to wake her mother. She didn't bother taking a shower. She was so tired, she took her clothes off and fell asleep in bed instantly.

Katie held her dress up, putting her face in the fabric. She could smell a faint trace of her perfume mixed in with his masculine scent. A tingle ran through her as memories of last night emerged. Chase, his firm hands cradling her head as their lips locked in a hungry kiss, his touch and caresses sending quivers through her body. She remembered the way he took her, insistent and sure, as if he had a right. But Katie sensed there was something else seething underneath his desire and need, and she wondered if it was anger or resentment, mixed with pain and grief... and tenderness.

"Hey, you coming?" Mary yelled, pounding on the closed bedroom door.

"You and Momma eat," Katie replied. "I'm going to take a shower."

Grabbing a clean towel, she got up and walked into the bathroom. She stared at the girl in the bathroom mirror. She almost didn't recognize herself—the smudged makeup around her eyes, smeared lipstick, messy and tangled hair. Katie put her finger tenderly on her mouth, tracing her puffy lips, and mouthed a silent thanks that Mary didn't barge in her room this morning.

Katie turned on the water, waited for it to warm up, and stepped into the shower. She shampooed her hair and squirted on extra conditioner. As she soaped and cleaned up, she wondered what Chase was thinking about last night and how much he had to drink at the wedding. What happened wasn't planned. Sex with Chase had always been wonderful. But last night had been different. Maybe her memories had faded in the last ten years. Perhaps her memories of last night were blurred, or she couldn't think clearly in the darkness under a faint moonlight.

She felt the heat on her cheeks as she washed, her body remembering where Chase had touched her last night, exploring places that hadn't been touched for a long time by a man. She remembered the way he ran his hands through her hair, the pressure of his lips, the raw longing in his eyes, the urgency of his desire. Her body quivered as if in response. She sighed, washing away the traces of his masculine scent, thinking it couldn't happen again. Last night was a mistake, right? The wedding and Kenny and Darlene—maybe it was all too much for Chase, knowing his brother would never be there to see Timmy grow up. Kenny and Darlene had missed his first birthday, his first steps, the first words out of his mouth, and the first day of school. And they would miss his first love, his graduation, his marriage, and everything in Timmy's life.

But she knew it was more than that. She saw the deep yearning in Chase's eyes, and for a moment, he'd opened his soul to her again, letting her catch a glimpse. Katie felt protected, loved, and invincible when he held her tight in his arms. She felt safe with him, the one person who would never push her away. When they became as one, it was the most exhilarating, euphoric feeling.

22

MARY AND MOMMA WERE SITTING AROUND THE KITCHEN table, finishing up their breakfast.

"Your food is on the stove," Mary said.

"Thank you." Katie grabbed a plate and dished out scrambled eggs from the frying pan and a heaping serving of creamy grits from the saucepan, adding extra pats of butter on top. She poured a full cup of coffee. Hands full, she carried it all to the table and sat down.

She didn't realize how famished she was until she took the first bite of eggs.

"This is delicious," she mumbled with her mouth full.

Mary laughed. "You don't know what you've been missing."

It didn't take long for Katie to scarf the food down. She finally put her fork down and pushed the plate away. She reached for the coffee cup and sat back in her chair, taking a long sip.

Momma had been quiet, watching Katie eat.

"You got in late last night." Her lips were pressed together.

"Yes, I let myself in."

"I waited for you for hours."

Katie felt like a kid again—a teenager being interrogated for missing curfew. Her dad had been strict when she was living at home. He had his rules and made sure she knew it. But Katie had a rebellious streak and ran past curfew more than a few times. He punished her for it and left her crying. Her momma had consoled her, wrapping Katie in her arms until the tears subsided.

She had disappointed her mother, and it was not a good feeling.

"I'm sorry. I didn't know you were waiting. Did I wake you up?"

"No, I went to bed. You know, I was worried."

"I'm a big girl now."

"So what happened?" Mary asked, leaning forward across the table.

Katie twisted her napkin, folded it, and unfolded it.

"Chase was going to take me straight home after the wedding, but I asked him to take a drive, and we made a couple of stops along the way."

"Must have been a long drive. You were gone for hours," Momma said.

"He took me to the new diner. Well, I know it's

been there a few years, but it was new to me. We had homemade custard pie. So yummy."

Momma cracked a smile.

"I remember how you taught us to cook. Remember the year we went apple picking and came back with bags full?" Katie asked.

She nodded.

"You took out pie pans while we washed the apples. I don't know how many apples we peeled and cut, but my hands were sore by the time we were done." Katie glanced at Mary, eyebrow raised.

"We had so much fun. And you let us roll the pastry. I made a mess and splattered flour all over," Mary said, a glint in her eye. "And you know what was the best part? When you opened the oven door, and I saw the beautiful pies—the first pies we made together."

Katie scanned the kitchen, the countertops, the stove, the oven. It was smaller than she'd remembered. But it held many memories—this kitchen and this small, humble house where she grew up. The chair where Dad had sat was now empty. She missed him. Momma was heartbroken when he died. He was the love of her life and her only one. Her grief was inconsolable. But Katie hadn't been here for her mom then, nor for her dad when he died. She'd put her career above everything and everyone else and paid a price for it. Mary had been here, and she'd shared what Momma had gone through—during the day when she stayed in the house, wanting to be left alone, and during the nights when she cried in bed, longing for her husband in the privacy of her bedroom. In the mornings, her eyes would be red and swollen.

Mary's voice broke in. "Momma has an eye appointment tomorrow morning."

"I'll take her," Katie offered.

"Can you? I thought you had a flight to catch." Mary frowned.

"What time is her appointment?"

"At ten."

"I can do it. My plane leaves later in the day. By the way, can you do me a favor and take me to the airport at five?"

"Sure."

"Okay, that's settled."

"So, what are you going to do today?" Mary asked.

"Dunno. Do you need help around the house?"

Mary rolled her eyes. "We could always use some, and we're getting a garage ramp built today."

Katie frowned, glancing at Mary and then back to Momma. "A ramp?"

"For Momma," Mary said. "She's having a bit of trouble getting around with the stairs."

"Does she have a wheelchair?"

"No, she doesn't need one now. She can use her walker, but if later she gets a wheelchair, then this ramp would be easier access to get from the car to inside the house and back outside."

"You have a carpenter?"

"Not exactly. Chase does this kind of handyman

work, and he's been helping and doing a few jobs here on weekends."

"I didn't know," Katie murmured, as a quickening stirred in her chest. She cleared her throat. "But doesn't he have to take care of Timmy?"

"Oh no, he brings Timmy. The kid loves it. He's a natural. You'll meet him."

"Chase had mentioned something about Timmy having a playdate yesterday and staying over with a friend. His face lit up when he talked about the child."

"Yeah, Chase has been doing a good job raising him. Timmy's turned out great. He's a nice kid. You'll see..."

23

KATIE PULLED ON A PAIR OF LONG, YELLOW GLOVES AND started washing the dishes. "You cooked. I'll clean."

Mary laughed as she cleared the table and brought the dirty plates, cups, and utensils to the sink. "Just like old times."

"It's the least I can do."

In twenty minutes, Katie had the dishes done and the kitchen sparkling clean. She went to her room to change into a fresh T-shirt and a pair of faded, tattered jeans. She tied her hair back in a ponytail and applied light eye shadow and a touch of lipstick. Eyeing herself in the mirror, she gave a nod of satisfaction, ignoring the fluttering feeling in her stomach and, at the same time, the thought of fleeing. She had entertained making an excuse to leave. But then, she'd be missing the chance to see Timmy, and she definitely wanted to meet this boy.

She heard the doorbell ring and Mary's voice call out in greeting.

It was time to go. She took one last look in the mirror and put on a smile.

She heard a child's voice talking to Mary as she walked into the living room. Then she saw him. A small boy, standing in front of Mary. His sandy hair was neatly trimmed and combed. He was dressed casually in a blue-and-white striped top, blue jeans, and sneakers.

Mary looked up and put a hand on his shoulder, pointing to Katie. "You haven't met my sister Katie."

Beaming, Katie bent her knees and stooped to the child's eye level. "Hi. You must be Timmy."

Timmy smiled and held himself straight, standing like a little man—a gentleman.

She held out her hand. "Nice to meet you."

He reached out, and his tiny hand clasped hers as they shook. "You have soft hands."

Katie couldn't resist giving him a hug, and her eyes met Chase, standing behind Timmy.

"I'm going to get started," Chase said, spinning around, one hand on the front doorknob.

"Would you like some help?" Katie asked.

"Not now; I'm unloading."

She turned to Timmy. "How about some hot chocolate?"

"Yes, ma'am," Timmy said, his eyes lighting up.

"Only if you call me Katie." She smiled and headed to the kitchen as the sounds of the TV blaring in the living room and Momma's laughing filled the air. Katie filled an electric kettle with water and turned it on. While it was heating, she selected a cup with cartoon characters from the cabinet, grabbed a packet of hot chocolate, and emptied it into the mug, keeping herself busy while her thoughts swirled. She knew about Timmy, but seeing him in person—her heart ached for this little guy who had lost both of his parents, standing tall before her, so polite and so brave.

The flip switch popped up, announcing the hot water was ready. Katie teared up, and her hands shook as she poured water into the mug, mixing the contents with a spoon before dropping the utensil in the sink. She turned around, hoping Timmy wouldn't notice her moistened eyes.

"Have a seat," Katie said as she pulled up a kitchen chair and sat, gesturing to Timmy. "I hope you like marshmallows." She set his cup on the table, the white nuggets floating at the top, their edges melting in the drink.

He nodded eagerly. "Oooh."

"Let it cool down for a bit."

Katie smiled, sliding a napkin across the table.

"You like helping Chase?"

"Yes. Chase is my uncle, but I call him Dad because he raised me."

"You want to be a carpenter when you grow up?"

"I wanna"—Timmy squirmed in his chair, wiggling his arm and pointing his finger at Katie—"drive those big trucks and lifts."

"A heavy-machine operator?"

"Yeah." Timmy waved, stretching his arms and making a wide half-circle in the air. "This big."

"That's cool."

Katie talked to Timmy and watched him slurp down his hot chocolate when it was ready to drink, finishing it off to the last drop.

Then he was done with talking. Timmy sat his empty mug down and slid off his chair. "I wanna go help Dad."

24

THE GARAGE DOOR WAS OPEN, THE INSIDE CLEARED except for the pile of lumber on the concrete floor to make the riser, ramp surface, and the posts and pieces for the handrail. A circular saw was plugged into a wall outlet, and an electric drill and boxes of nails sat next to it.

Chase looked up as Timmy bounced into sight, Katie closely following.

"He wanted to help..." Katie said, her voice lamely trailing. She skidded to a stop, surveying the materials spread on the ground. "Where are you building the ramp?"

"I'll attach the ramp to the landing here, which is flush with the door threshold." Chase walked over to the door that opened into the garage, pointing to the existing landing and the two stairs. He knocked on the outer wood railing. "And I'll remove this handrail to create the ramp access, while the other handrail attached to the wall remains. The ramp will also have these rails, with one against the wall."

"It'll be wider than the steps," Katie observed from a closer distance.

"And safer."

They were interrupted by a grunt and a yell in quick succession as Timmy struggled to pick up a piece of wood before dropping it on the concrete, making a loud thunk.

Chase rushed over to a red-faced Timmy. "Are you okay?"

"I just wanna help."

"This piece is too heavy for you." Chase picked up a shorter, lighter piece of wood. "Tell you what... can you handle these short spindles for the handrail?"

Timmy reached for it, and grinned when he succeeded.

"Okay then, can you bring them over there to the garage stairs?"

"Yeah."

"Good," Chase said, patting the child's back. "You're a big help."

"What can I do?" Katie asked.

"How about you hand the pieces to me when I need them, except for those heavy ones?" Chase glanced at the largest pieces of lumber.

THE THREE OF them worked steadily and in rhythm. Katie stole side glances at Chase out of the corner of her eyes as he busied himself with measuring and marking, cutting wood, and driving in screws.

She couldn't help thinking about last night. Did it really happen? Or was it a figment of her imagination and lust? It took all her will to act naturally in the presence of little Timmy and her family. Since Chase had arrived, they hadn't had a chance to be alone—not even for a minute. She wasn't going to bring it up. She considered it, wondering if it was even wise, and if she did, what would she say? They'd had a future together and had talked about it and planned for it—a long time ago. Katie blamed herself for not reaching out, but her pride had held her back. She had broken up with Chase, and she wouldn't be the one to call or beg him to come back. She had pushed it out of her mind and turned off the replay button. She still had memories, but they were archived when it concerned the two of them.

She hid a smile, bending her head down as last night's memories flooded her thoughts unbidden. These recent memories were still fresh, and she couldn't shake them off yet—and didn't want to.

CHASE HARDLY TALKED while he was working on building the ramp. He'd explained to them he needed to concentrate, especially when taking measurements and cutting. It was true. But he knew he was putting off the inevitable, and Katie was bound to bring up last night.

In the bright light of day, he tried to make sense of the night before—those emotions gripped him so powerfully, churning and playing with his heart, heating to new heights under the light of the moon. He felt as if he were under a spell, and there was no way out except one. The pull was magical as he gazed deeply into her soft eyes, inhaled her maddening scent, and cradled his head in the valley of her chest as she wrapped her arms tightly around him, not letting him go.

He shook his head to clear his thoughts. Nope, he wasn't going down this path again. He'd learned his lesson. Ten years without hearing a single word from Katie, and now, she'd shown up again. Resentment crept back in. He'd given her his love once, but she'd dropped him cold and cut up his heart into pieces. It'd taken almost all this time to forget and patch his broken heart. He'd vowed he'd never let her hurt him again. The bitterness had left an ugly taste in his mouth.

It was Timmy who had healed him—the innocence and love of this child had given Chase the ability to love again. More than anyone in this world, Timmy had opened his heart.

25

CHASE FINISHED THE RAMP AT THE END OF THE LONG DAY. He nodded in satisfaction at his handiwork.

He gathered the materials and cleaned up the job site, using a broom and dustpan leaning against a corner of the garage and some trash bags. Hours ago, he'd sent Katie and Timmy inside. He'd taken a couple of quick bathroom breaks and checked to see what they were doing, pleased to see them playing games with Mary.

"Wow, it's done." Mary had popped her head in the garage intermittently throughout his work, and had done it with more frequency in the last hour.

"Yep. You want to try it out first?" Chase asked.

"I'm going to get Momma," she said, disappearing again.

He could hear her in the house, hollering excitedly for Katie and Timmy to join her.

A few minutes later, their momma stepped out onto the landing, a daughter on each side, holding on to her arms. Her eyes twinkled with delight. "I'm going to walk it alone," she said, a girlish lilt in her voice as she shrugged her arms free and stepped on the ramp.

All eyes were on Momma as she made her way down slowly, a step at a time, her hand firmly on the side rail. When her feet finally touched the concrete garage floor, she walked up to Chase.

"Well done. Thank you," she said.

"You're welcome." Chase grinned almost from ear to ear.

"Would you join me for the walk back up the ramp?"

"I'd be delighted and honored." He raised his arm, crooking his elbow.

She rested her arm on his, and her other hand grasped the handrail as they walked up on the ramp.

A rousing cheer met their eardrums as they reached the top landing. A round of hugs followed.

"Now, let's go inside and eat." Momma stepped over the threshold.

"What's for dinner?" Timmy piped up.

"Your favorite—chicken 'n' dumplings," Momma said, ruffling his hair.

THE FLAVORFUL POT of chicken broth with sautéed celery and onions, cut-up chicken, and plump dollops of round drop dumplings seasoned with herbs and spices had been simmering for hours on the stove. Their momma knew Katie didn't eat meat, so she made a separate pot using vegetable broth instead, adding the same sautéed vegetables and dumplings, but without the chicken. She also prepared a large bowl of fresh green salad with lettuce, cherry tomatoes, sliced cucumbers, red onions, and hard-boiled eggs.

The delicious smell emanating from the kitchen brought on a sudden pang of hunger as Chase quickly washed up, working up a rich lather of soap on his hands. Katie was setting the table, and Timmy was helping her.

When they were all seated, Mary dished out generous servings of the chicken 'n' dumplings in large bowls and passed them to everyone except Katie, who had gotten up to serve herself, filling her bowl from another pot on the stove.

"What are you eating?" asked Timmy, who was sitting next to Katie, noticing she wasn't getting the same food in her bowl.

"Dumplings without the chicken. I don't eat meat," Katie said, swirling her spoon in the broth to show him it didn't have any chicken.

"Ooh," Timmy said. He wrinkled his nose. "You don't like chicken?"

"I used to eat chicken, grew up with it. But after I moved to the city, I changed my diet and quit eating beef, pork, and chicken."

He frowned. "Really?"

"People have choices—we can dress, talk, and eat differently. But I wouldn't force my preferences on you or anyone else. And I wouldn't like it if someone forced me."

"To each his own," Mary said, passing the salad bowl.

"I don't know about you, but I'm famished," Chase said, raising a spoonful of the chicken 'n' dumplings to his mouth. A smile crossed his lips as he savored the mouthful. He turned to Momma. "Thank you, ma'am. This is mighty fine homemade chicken 'n' dumplings. Best I've ever had."

"There's plenty more where that comes from," she said, beaming.

A loud slurp and clinking got everyone's attention as Timmy got busy, digging into his bowl.

"Yummy, huh?" Chase said.

Timmy looked up, bits of creamy dumpling clinging to the edge of his lips, and nodded.

After the meal, Katie and Mary washed the dishes. Chase offered to help, but they shooed him away.

He waited until they were done cleaning up before saying, "It's Timmy's bedtime."

Timmy groaned. "Do we have to go?"

"I'm afraid so. You've got school tomorrow."

"And Katie is leaving tomorrow," Mary said, wiping her hands dry on the kitchen towel.

Chase raised his eyebrows.

"I'm catching a flight in the evening. I've got to get back to work," Katie said. Her eyes met Chase's, and a flicker passed between them. She looked away, her chin trembling.

26

It had been a long day. On the drive home, Chase noticed Timmy was getting sleepy, with his belly full of good food. He left him alone.

He sighed, feeling worn out and beat. His muscles would be sore tomorrow, but it wasn't just his body. Chase felt a weariness all over and a heaviness in his chest. The weight of it was dragging him down, and with it, he was losing hope.

The short drive took about five minutes. He pulled into his driveway. Timmy had been quiet, having fallen asleep. Chase shook him gently, and when the child didn't respond, he got Timmy ready for bed, stripping off his shoes, socks, shirt, and pants, pulling on his PJs, and tucking him in bed without a bath. He leaned over and kissed Timmy gently on his cheek, but the child was snoring.

Chase took a hot shower, washing away the day's grunge. He went to bed, sinking into the puffy pillow.

Sleep didn't come. He got up to get a drink of water in the kitchen and paced in the living room. Settling on the couch, he turned on the TV, fingers working the remote, clicking on random channels aimlessly, with nothing specific in mind. He skipped the ads, becoming aware the volume went up when the ad played and then lowered when it went back to regular programming. The loud sound was grinding, harsh, and irritating. His head throbbed, but rubbing his temples and the tight muscles in his neck didn't help. In a fit, he turned off the TV and tossed the remote.

He sat on the couch, bristling, surrounded by silence. His thoughts turned to Katie—not the Katie from yesterday, but the one today. She hadn't said one word to him about last night, but acted normal, like nothing had happened. She didn't even mention she'd be leaving tomorrow. If it wasn't for Mary, he'd never have known. The bitterness crept in. He clenched his teeth, tightening his jaw muscles. Chase went over the day, each interaction they had. She had kept her distance, but it wasn't obvious she was avoiding him. He could tell the difference—or thought he could.

He stared at the living room wall, the one he'd painted beige, as if he could find an answer there. He wondered if he'd misinterpreted her actions. Twice, he'd lingered at the kitchen sink while Katie was washing dishes, hoping to catch a moment alone with her. He had moved closer, under the guise of bringing his dirty dishes to the sink. But Mary had shooed him away, saying he didn't need to help. Had Katie confided in her? Perhaps not. He had detected no change in Mary. If she'd known, she might have even teased him a bit 'cause she couldn't resist.

He didn't know Katie was leaving tomorrow. If he had, he'd have tried harder to talk to her about last night. Was she playing with his feelings? His pulse quickened as he remembered. He had felt something. What stirred inside of him wasn't just lust and longing, although she had that effect on him. Every time. He'd slipped and let her get close to him again. Not just physically, but she occupied his mind, too. He couldn't get her out of his thoughts. He needed to clear his head, and he didn't know how. Tomorrow, she'd be leaving town and out of his life again. He wanted to—no, *they* needed to talk. He couldn't let her go without resolution. Life was different now. He'd made a home with Timmy.

KATIE PACKED her suitcase for the next day before she went to bed. She had promised to take Momma to the doctor in the morning, and then they'd have lunch together. This weekend was almost over. Her thoughts drifted back to Chase and meeting Timmy. Seeing them together and how happy they were brought a lump to her throat. She liked the boy instantly, and he'd carved out a special place in her heart. They had broken bread together, sharing a delicious homemade meal and lots of laughs tonight—like one big, happy family.

But she'd ruined it. Torn it up and ripped it apart all by herself. She had distanced herself, acted aloof, and withheld information from Chase she shouldn't have. It was hindsight now, a little too late. She was sorry for not telling Chase she was leaving tomorrow. Her heart ached, seeing the look on his face—the shock of finding out from Mary that Katie was going back home. His eyes had dulled, the light and gleam snubbed out. She saw the change as the glow disappeared, replaced by hurt and disappointment. And suppressed anger. The glance they'd exchanged confirmed it.

Perhaps he thought she'd changed. Perhaps she used him last night. Could she have been so cruel? She could have apologized and lightened the pain she caused, but she didn't. She let Chase walk out of the house and out of her life again. Katie sighed, breathing deeply. The sad part was she didn't even say a proper goodbye to Timmy. He deserved more from her. Both of them did.

27

THE RESTFUL SLEEP KATIE CRAVED CAME IN THE WEE hours of the morning as exhaustion finally took over. She'd set the alarm on her phone for eight-thirty, with enough time to get up, eat breakfast, and have everything ready to take Momma to the eye doctor.

Katie tapped the snooze button when the alarm sounded and fell back on the pillow, lingering for a minute, her eyes wide open. The sunlight streamed in through the thin curtains as the shadows retreated. She took comfort in the familiar surroundings, where she'd spent her whole life until she left town after high school. This was her sanctuary, where she retreated when she wanted to be alone. Where Katie had laughed and cried and dreamed of doing bigger things in life, and it was here the seed germinated to leave her family, home, town, and Chase, the first love of her life. It'd been a scary thought, and she'd shoved it away, cramming it down. But she'd become restless, obsessed, fueled with energy she didn't know she had.

Jumping out of bed, she dressed slowly, taking a long look around as if memorizing the furniture, the walls, and the items in the room she fondly remembered, making a mental snapshot again before another farewell.

Katie eyed the tired linoleum flooring as she walked into the kitchen to start breakfast. It had looked the same ever since she could remember. The clunky cookie jar on the countertop with a chip on the lid where she'd dropped it, the bread box dinged with use, the cabinet door with its handle sticky with greasy grime. It was funny, she thought, how these details didn't bother her as a kid, but seeing them now, her stomach twisted.

Dad had promised Momma he'd upgrade the kitchen, knowing how much she loved to cook. But as the years went by, money was still tight. Momma saved and scraped and stretched the grocery money as far as she could, buying packaged food, snacks, and drinks at the dollar store. But other needs always came up. It had been the medical bills and prescription costs when Dad was sick, and fixing the car, which had more and more problems as it got older. And there had been the upkeep on the house. Although they saved some money in their rainy-day funds, the meager savings were near depleted to pay off the bills and rising cost-of-living expenses. Katie hadn't realized how hard life had been for her parents. They didn't complain. She had never heard them.

Momma had aged; the lines had drawn deeper as her skin sagged. The last few years had been hard. Since Dad passed away, it'd been a struggle for her. It was grief and the shock of losing her mate for life. She'd gradually lost interest in cooking. Mary would visit whenever she could, and they'd cook and eat together, but she had her own life to live, and it was a busy one.

Katie regretted not coming home more often, especially toward the end of her father's life when he was sick. And she wasn't by his side when he died. Momma was at his bedside, and so was Mary, when he took his last breath.

Momma hadn't been eating a large breakfast. But she loved her caffeine and orange juice. Katie made a pot of strong, dark coffee, poured a steaming cup for her mom, and set it, along with a glass of juice, on the table. She added oil to the frying pan on the stove and cracked eggs. While they were sizzling in the pan, she popped two slices of bread in the toaster.

When everything was ready, Katie went to get Momma. She knocked on her bedroom door. "Breakfast is ready." It was the least she could do, fix a simple breakfast that took her a few minutes to make.

When she was a little girl, Momma was always the first one up, but Mary had mentioned she seemed more tired lately and lacked the energy she used to have. Momma was not well, but she didn't let on.

There was some shuffling, then creaking of the wooden floorboards.

"Something smells good." Momma sniffed as she opened the door.

"Did you sleep well?"

"I got about five hours."

"Not enough?"

"It'll have to do."

They walked back to the kitchen, and Katie dragged out a chair in front of her place setting on the table. "Come and sit. Is this okay? I can whip up some pancakes if you'd like."

"It's fine. Lord knows my appetite isn't what it used to be."

"You feeling all right?"

"Old age soreness. My body's falling apart."

"After we eat, we'll make sure your eyes get checked out."

"And next week's my dentist appointment."

"Regular visit?"

"My twice-a-year cleaning."

"What do you want to do after lunch?"

"Aren't you leaving today?" Momma asked, raising her eyebrow.

"Yes, my flight leaves in the evening. I have a few hours to spare."

"Don't you worry about me. Isn't there something you need to do, hon?"

"I'm all yours, Momma." Katie flashed a smile, putting on a brave front. She had something she needed to do—apologize to Chase. But she couldn't say it out loud or admit it to herself. Katie didn't feel like talking about it to her mother, not now. Maybe it'd make it worse, seeing him before she left. Katie gritted her teeth. She'd loved him once, long ago, and broke his heart then. She did it again yesterday, here in this very house. How could she forget the stunned look on his face, the slump of his shoulders? Yet Chase had murmured to her, "Have a safe trip," on his way out the door.

28

THE DOCTOR'S OFFICE WAS ON MAIN STREET, A SHORT distance from Momma's house. Katie thought of the sprawling city she lived in and how far she had to drive to get to places. The traffic was a nightmare, especially around rush hour—except it wasn't just an hour, but more like two to three hours.

She'd inherited her thriftiness from Momma. Katie lived in a small apartment in a complex with a common green space. It was the one thing that was non-negotiable when she looked for a place to live. Having a granite countertop kitchen, fancy bathroom, or a stylish building wasn't a big deal for her. But that piece of green made it feel like home. And it was a welcome sight, her piece of heaven, after a long day at work. If she had to stare at slabs of concrete instead, it'd be so depressing.

Katie had carved out a life in the city and a routine

consisting of working late, grabbing fast food or settling for a frozen dinner, checking work emails on her laptop, showering, and sleeping. Then repeat the next day and the day after. On weekends, she did her chores, laundry, shopping, and errands.

She was often too tired to go out on Friday nights. The only exception was work-related social events, which she felt obligated to attend. If she had a date or went out with friends, it was on Saturday night. She had little free time. Her friends had to literally drag her out, or else she'd still be working, even on the weekends when she brought work home. They kidded her, too, and said she was married to her job.

She heard some grumblings after she got the big promotion. It was fair to say nobody envied her when she was at the bottom of the ladder, but she didn't stay there long. Katie had to work twice as hard as any man and work smarter. She was good at what she did. When she earned her way to success, she also earned the respect of her male colleagues. But she found out the hard way that some women resented her success, especially the one woman who made life most difficult for her on purpose.

She was still fuming when Momma directed her from the passenger seat, "Make a left turn there to the doctor's office."

She parked and walked around to help Momma out, but she waved her off, muttering that she was quite capable of it herself. Katie waited, standing in the parking lot and surveying the one-story, neatly painted house. "This place hasn't changed a bit."

"It's been this way ever since Doc Judy opened the practice over thirty years ago."

"I remember. You took me here to get my first glasses."

"You were in second or third grade?"

"Third. I didn't know I needed them until they gave us eye and hearing tests at school."

"And you rebelled. Stamped your tiny feet and said they looked ridiculous."

"Well, I didn't want those ugly black frames."

"But when Doc Judy pulled out those pink ones and said she'd saved them just for you, that did the trick."

"They were so cute! I got a pink lollipop, too, that day." Katie burst out laughing, then checked her phone. "Mom, it's almost time for your appointment. Shall we go in now?"

"I'll go. Why don't you wait outside or walk around? You'll get bored in the waiting room. I'll see you when I'm done."

Katie nodded and waited until she disappeared inside the building. She strolled leisurely down to the sidewalk and picked a bench to sit on and enjoy the sunshine and do some people watching. At this time of the day, most of the pedestrians were elderly townsfolk out and about, getting their exercise, walking and stopping to chat with people they knew. She didn't see kids who were in school and working-age adults who were too busy during the day to be loitering.

Along the street, she glimpsed a flower shop, a lawyer's office, and a clothing store. Farther down were the dry cleaner and hair salon. Other shops stretched beyond her line of vision.

Across from her, the shiny bank building stood in a central location on Main Street. To its right stood an old-fashioned drugstore. Inside, the pharmacy and shelves filled with sundries took half of the space, and the soda fountain and dining area, famous for its malt shakes and faux-red-leather booths, occupied the other half. It was a popular gathering place for retirees who picked up their prescription medications and loitered, meeting up with people they knew for a drink or a meal served at the counter or booths.

An elderly woman exited the pharmacy and crossed the street. As the woman approached the bench where she was sitting, Katie recognized her former second-grade teacher, Mrs. Bell, and almost ducked like a kid playing hooky from school.

Now white-haired and walking with a slight stoop, this woman differed from the Mrs. Bell that Katie remembered—a stern, middle-aged teacher, taking no flak from any of her students when they misbehaved. If a kid wasn't paying attention in class, she'd go around with the pointer and rap it hard on the wooden desk, making loud thwacks when metal met wood, shocking whoever was sitting there to attention. It was effective, though, and did the job... enough to wipe the smirk off a kid's face and make them sit up and listen. She remembered her dedication and soft side, too, when Mrs. Bell spent hours helping the struggling students like her who strived to succeed.

"Well, if it isn't Katie Simmons." Mrs. Bell was standing inches away, peering down at her former student through her bifocal glasses.

Katie squirmed and looked up into those no-nonsense gray eyes. "Mrs. Bell. I'm so surprised to see you." She stood up to greet her, brushing her pants to wipe away some imagined fluff.

"Have you moved back to town?"

"No. I was just in town for the weekend to attend a wedding." She tilted her head toward Doc Judy's place. "Waiting for my mom, then flying out today."

"Young lady, I hear you've got a busy career, but we don't see much of you."

Katie blushed. "I applied what you taught me, you know, and worked really hard."

Mrs. Bell's lips upturned in a terse smile. "And you've accomplished a lot. Are you happy now?"

"I thought it was what I wanted, more than anything. I left everything behind and everyone I loved to pursue my goal in the city."

"But you didn't answer my question—are you happy?"

"No," Katie said in a quiet whisper, her shoulders sagging. Back in high school, she had dreams of making it big in the city and having it all. But she had let go of Chase. Cut the ties all by herself. She had a nice nest egg and a job she'd climbed the ladder to get. She didn't need more money. Heck, she was making more than anyone in her family ever had. In one fell swoop, Mrs. Bell had asked about the one thing she didn't have. The one thing money couldn't buy, no matter how high she reached or how many achievements and accolades she accumulated. The one thing she'd let go.

She'd settled for the life she had now. Convinced herself it was a full life, filling her time to the brim every day. She'd smile and go to work every morning, while the knot in her belly tightened a little bit more each day. She was good at hiding the emptiness inside. Nobody had guessed. She'd held it in, kept it to herself.

At night, she'd take off her cheerful face and stop acting. Scrub off her makeup and shower, then get in bed and hug her pillow.

She remembered when she frolicked and romped in the field with Chase. Carefree and barefoot, they'd run, jump, and dance in the tall grass, laughing and squealing. One day, he had plucked a bouquet of beautiful wildflowers, and with the earnest face and the innocence of a child, he'd asked her, "Will you be mine?"

For an answer, she'd kissed him on his soft lips.

"Katie?" Mrs. Bell asked, interrupting her thoughts.

She blinked and let out a long exhale, running her fingers through her hair.

"You okay?"

Katie bowed her head, but not before Mrs. Bell caught sight of her forlorn expression.

Mrs. Bell squeezed her shoulder. "Some things are worth holding on to. You just have to figure out what you want."

29

Chase wanted to take the day off and crawl back in bed. But he didn't. He got Timmy off to school and arrived at work at the bank, passing by people without stopping to talk, going directly into his office and shutting the door.

He went through the routine, turned on his computer, checked his emails, and listened to his voicemails. Chase plowed through work, forgoing a trip to the break room for his coffee, where he'd have to chat with anyone he ran into. He concentrated on the tasks at hand, avoiding distractions, shutting out thoughts of Katie.

Working furiously nonstop until midmorning, Chase finally pushed his keyboard off to the side, massaging his temples to find relief for the tension headache throbbing relentlessly. He stood up and stretched, walking around his desk to look out the enormous window facing Main Street. He had a magnificent view. The office was a perk he appreciated, overlooking the street in front of the bank.

It was sunny, the world outside so different from the darkened, air-conditioned office he was working in. Neat sidewalks on the cleanest curbs, colorful signs and store displays, water bowls for dogs next to doorways, people walking leisurely as if they had all the time in the world, stopping to talk now and then. He caught a splash of color across the street, the shirt or outfit of someone sitting on the bench enjoying the day, and almost wished he didn't have to work, like the person wearing the brightly colored clothes. But there was something familiar about the figure. He squinted his eyes, glimpsing the face—Katie's face—as it turned straight toward him, gazing at the bank.

His pulse quickened, and blood rushed through his veins. Did she spot him? Could she see inside the building from across the street?

Chase stepped back, jerking his body away from the window. He'd shoved her out of his mind, and here she was—in the flesh. He groaned. This wasn't what he expected. He eased forward again, eyes focused on Katie. Was she thinking of him, sitting there on the bench? Was that why she picked the spot? Was she hoping to see him before she left town again? He swallowed. Would she get up and come to the bank to see him?

Then he couldn't see her anymore. Someone had blocked the view, and all he could see was a larger figure dressed in a flowery dress, talking to Katie and hugging her. He stared at the woman as he realized it was her mother. She pointed at the drugstore. Katie nodded, and the two of them started walking across the street.

Without warning, suddenly, a dog barked as it ran into the street in their direction, startling Katie's mother. Mrs. Simmons darted to her right, trying to skirt around the dog and move out of the way. She lost her balance and footing and fell.

Chase sprang into action and rushed out of the bank. By the time he reached her, Mrs. Simmons was down on the ground and gripping her leg.

Katie was bent over, knees digging into the asphalt, clutching her hand. "Mom, are you hurt?"

Her leg was turned out on the side that hit the pavement. She tried to get up, extending her arm and holding on to Katie for support. Her face red with exertion, she used her other arm to prop her body up and raise it. Chase could see the pain etched on her face as she tried to put weight on her leg to get up. She let go, sinking back on the ground and panting with the effort, one hand placed on her hip.

"Don't stand. Let's get you checked out first," Chase said.

He whipped out his cell phone and dialed, putting it on speakerphone so Katie and her mother could hear.

"Nine-one-one. What's your emergency?"

"Ma'am, we need an ambulance."

"What's your name?"

"Chase Beard."

"Can you tell me what happened?"

"We have an injured person on the street."

"What's your location?"

"Main Street. Across from the bank."

"Tell me what happened."

"It's Mrs. Simmons; she fell on the pavement." Chase kneeled down quickly, almost butting heads with Katie. Her mother was moaning softly. "She's in pain. Please send help."

It didn't take long for the ambulance to show up. The hospital was close by. Two EMTs in uniform responded to the scene, then wheeled out a stretcher, carefully lifting Mrs. Simmons onto it and rolling her into the vehicle.

Katie was pacing back and forth, a strained look on her face. Chase gently touched her arm. She paused, wrinkling her brow.

"I'm going to follow the ambulance. Would you like a ride?" he asked.

She fumbled with her purse, pinching the zipper tab and grasping the strap. Her eyes darted, flitting around. "Where's your car?"

Chase waved toward the bank. "Over there—it's the silver SUV. I don't usually drive my truck to work." His eyes caught her gaze, full of worry. He wanted to calm and reassure her. To wrap her in his arms and comfort her. Wordlessly, he glanced to make sure no traffic was coming and pulled her across the street to his car. She didn't protest.

Once they were both sitting in the SUV and buckled up, he started it and backed up, then turned the wheel and whipped out of the parking lot, speeding after the ambulance.

Her hands still shaky, Katie pulled out her cell phone.

He could hear her side of the conversation, telling her sister about the fall and where they were going before she ended the call.

Her head sank back on the headrest, eyes closed.

Chase let her be as he focused on driving, maneuvering through traffic and turning into the hospital parking lot. He could see the ambulance had parked in front of the emergency doors, and the EMTs were taking Mrs. Simmons inside on the stretcher.

He hurried to park and turned the engine off. Katie's eyes were still closed. He rubbed her arm, watching as her eyes popped open. "We need to go," he urged, opening his door and hopping out. He slammed his door and ran around to her side.

"I'm not an invalid," she said, lips pressed together.

He held out both his hands, palms facing out in a hands-off pose. When she got out of the car, he nudged her arm to walk faster inside.

30

Katie didn't mean to snipe at Chase when he offered his hand to her when she exited the car. She regretted it instantly. Blaming it on her nerves wasn't a good excuse. She liked his take-charge attitude.

At work, Katie was the one who made decisions and gave the orders. But she froze today, seeing her mother lying awkwardly on the pavement. It shocked her to witness Momma in a twisted position, vulnerable and in pain. The strong woman who had raised her was not the person before her now, unable to get up and move. A minute before, they were heading toward the soda fountain for a luscious malt and excited about spending some time together and enjoying a meal before her flight left. In a flash, it had all changed.

She knew Chase worked at the bank and had entertained thoughts of seeing him. She'd scanned the building hoping to spot him. But she hadn't gone to seek him out. Had he been watching her? Did he see Momma fall? Chase had come running, rushing out to be at their side. She couldn't help noticing how handsome he looked in a suit. Chase had acted assertively, calling 911 and getting her mother to the hospital. He got her there, too, following the ambulance to the emergency room. He was calm, assured, and quick-thinking. She was glad to see him and grateful for his help.

They were sitting in the waiting room, their chairs side by side. The doctors had examined Momma, and someone had taken her to radiology for X-rays and an MRI. Chase got up and excused himself, holding his phone in his hand. Katie swallowed. Was he leaving to go back to work? She'd be left alone for a few hours until Mary's shift at the restaurant ended and she could come to the hospital.

Katie hoped he wasn't leaving. She shifted and readjusted her position, picking up a magazine to read. She didn't hear him walk up to her until she saw his shoes appear in her line of vision. Katie looked up, eye-level to the two paper cups he was holding in front of her.

"Coffee?"

She reached out for a cup, the liquid inside a pale brown. "Thank you."

"If you don't like it, there's also hot chocolate."

"No, this is fine." She sipped the coffee, raising an eyebrow at the weak and watered-down brew.

"Vending machine special." He smiled, sitting back down in the chair.

"Okay." She nursed the cup in her hand, swirling the liquid. "Are you going back to work?"

"No, not yet."

"I—I appreciate your help. I'm sorry for sniping at you earlier."

She heard him murmuring something about it being no big deal and about being available to stay longer should she need him. "Mary will be here after her shift ends. She's going home to change and then to go get Jim before she comes here. You gonna pick Timmy up after school?"

"Yes, I'm going to go to his school and take him home, and I've made arrangements for a sitter to come later."

She shot up straight. She'd been so busy thinking about everybody else, she'd forgotten about her flight this evening. What was wrong with her? She had to be back at work in the morning, right? She rummaged through her purse, frantically searching for the plane ticket. Her fingertips found it, and she plucked it out. She skimmed through the ticket for the flight information, confirming her departure time wasn't until this evening. Sally, her assistant, had made the reservations.

"Would you excuse me? I've got a call to make." She rose, ticket in one hand and her phone in the other, and scurried out of the room toward the hallway.

Sally answered on the first ring.

"Hi, Katie here. Do you have a moment?"

"Yeah, what's up?"

"I really need your help. Can you please cancel my flight today?"

"Oh, are you okay?"

"Yes. I—we have a family emergency, and I need to stay here."

"Gosh, I'm so sorry. You want me to schedule a return flight for another day?"

"I don't know yet. I'll need to call you later." Katie paused. "Can you transfer me to Joanne?"

"Sure, I'll put you on hold."

"You're the best. Thank you."

The last person Katie wanted to talk to was Joanne, the BFH. She bit her lip as she waited, counting the number of rings, hoping the call would go straight to her voicemail. When her prerecorded greeting played, she left a quick message, repeating what she'd told Sally, and ended the call.

She leaned her back against the hallway wall, grateful for the solid support. Her stomach churned, and she felt a tightness in her chest. Would Joanne go ballistic? Give her hell? There was no telling what she'd do. One thing was for sure: That woman didn't have a sympathetic ear or a kind bone in her body. She breathed slowly, inhaling and exhaling a long breath.

The hallway door swooshed open. She turned her head to see Chase running out, the soles of his shoes squishing on the smooth, waxed floor.

"The doctor wants to talk to you now," he said,

waving in the direction of the waiting room as he spun around.

She dropped her ticket and phone in her purse and snapped it shut.

31

KATIE SPRINTED AFTER HIM, HEART POUNDING. WHAT would the doctor say about Momma?

Chase had stopped in front of a distinguished-looking, silver-haired man dressed in scrubs and a white coat.

As she approached him, she could read his name tag: Sean Fallon, MD.

"Hi, I'm Dr. Fallon. You are Mrs. Simmons's daughter?"

She nodded. "Yes, one of her two daughters. I'm Katie. Pleased to meet you, doctor."

"Your mother is being prepped for surgery."

Katie looked from Chase to the doctor, frowning. "What's wrong?"

"She has a fractured hip. She's going to need a hip repair to fix it."

Katie sucked in her breath, covering her mouth with her palm. "Oh no."

"We'll need to put the pieces back together. The fracture is along the upper femur. We'll put a rod in the bone shaft and use pins or screws to attach it to the hip and to hold them together in place while it heals."

She must have made a sour face. The doctor replied sympathetically, "The good news is your mother won't be needing a hip replacement."

"This—this doesn't sound as bad." A brief smile upturned her lips. "Doctor, how long will the surgery take?"

"Two to four hours. She'll be sore and on pain meds after."

"Will she be staying in the hospital for a while?"

"She'll have to stay for two or three days, and we'll be monitoring her closely. But she's going to need help at home." He gave her a stern nod and turned to go.

"Thank you, Dr. Fallon."

CHASE THOUGHT he could put her out of his mind, once and for all.

Katie was standing so close, his heart raced. He hadn't expected to see her today. She was taking deep breaths, the rise and fall of her chest gradually slowing down as her fists unclenched. His heart softened to see her like this. His thoughts jumped wildly. If only he could help her. If only she'd let him.

She had come back into his life a grown woman who'd carved out a place for herself, doing it the way she'd dreamed of. She was strong, determined, and capable. But seeing her like this, so vulnerable and worried, he wanted nothing more than to protect her. To let her know he would not abandon her, even though he'd been hurt.

"Would you like to sit?" he said.

Her beautiful hazel eyes met his.

Chase swallowed, wondering if she knew his heart was pounding now. Inside, he was that boy again. Shy, awkward, and naïve. He'd been in love with her and carried the flame for her until she snubbed it out. But he'd dug through the embers and found his broken heart, keeping it buried and yet not extinguished. He had no assurance one day things would change. Would she look at him again the way she used to?

"Sit?" Katie surveyed the waiting room, looking at the empty chairs and those occupied by the people sitting scattered around the room. In the corner, an old man dozed with his mouth open, a drizzle of saliva dangling from his lip and dribbling down to his chin. Off to the side, a couple murmured in each other's ears and nestled so close, their arms were intertwined. Further down sat a young mother carrying her sleeping baby in a sling.

Chase checked the time. "We have at least a couple of hours."

"I'd like some fresh air. It's too depressing in here."

"Don't you have to wait for Mary?"

"She'll be here after her shift ends, but she's going

home first to change and then pick Jim up. She'll call me when she's on her way."

"C'mon. I'll walk out with you. There's nothing we can do now while she's in surgery." He wanted desperately to have a talk with her.

"You're leaving?" Katie asked, her voice dropping to a whisper as they walked out into the bright sunshine.

"I have to pick up Timmy."

"Oh, yes." She shuffled her feet. "I forgot about it. I don't know when I'll see him again." Chase saw a bitter smile flicker on her face.

He stepped in front of her and tilted her chin up. "Look at me." Her eyes made brief contact, then broke away. "I can explain it to Timmy. You don't have to be so hard on yourself."

"You've done a wonderful job raising him. As both mother and father. I didn't even take care of my own parents."

"It's not too late."

"I'm not saying I regret everything I've done. Part of me knows my dad was proud of me. He believed in me and supported me going after my dreams. The money he and Momma saved, well, they helped to pay for my college expenses." She paused, wiping a tear from her damp cheek. "You've seen their house and how frugally they lived..."

He felt the urge to hug her tight. Tell her it wasn't too late. For her dad, yes, but not for her momma. Not for her sister. Not for him. But he didn't.

"I'm sorry," she said.

He'd dreamed of revenge for years, thinking of what he'd do to the woman who'd spurned him. Those feelings were once powerful, first the love and then the bitterness that pushed out the sweetness. Did she pity him?

"That's why you made love to me? You felt sorry for me?"

Her eyes widened. "Oh, no. It... it's not what you're thinking."

"Then why toy with my feelings again?"

She leaned forward, eyes flashing close to his face. "No, I wasn't playing with you." Then her voice softened, and tenderness crept in. "Don't you know, Chase?"

He knew that day when he plucked the bouquet of wildflowers for her. He knew on their first date. He knew later, after their kiss. He knew at Laurie's wedding. He couldn't resist her—not now, or ever. He'd kissed other women and dated in the last ten years. But mostly, they were brief encounters. None of them made his heart beat the way Katie did. He knew what they had together, what they talked about, what they once shared. He knew her. He knew she loved him. Once long ago. And maybe still.

32

Katie had said yes when Chase asked her to ride along to pick up Timmy. He explained that he usually took Timmy to the bus stop in the morning, but he liked to pick the boy up after school. They often stopped at the store on the way back to buy groceries or get school supplies or materials for a homework project. On special days, they'd get a treat.

He pulled up in front of the elementary school and parked just as the bell rang and the kids were let out.

"Remember when we used to go here?" she asked, rolling down the window, listening to the kids laughing and calling out to each other as they stormed out.

"Yeah."

"I thought people our age were old. But I couldn't wait to grow up." She watched as the children ran and jumped, their short legs flying. Some kids dumped their backpacks on the front lawn to play. Others walked toward the idling school buses waiting in a line.

Chase was already out of the car, dashing across the school grounds, when Timmy spotted him and yelled. He turned as the boy flew into his arms, and they hugged, happy to see each other.

Katie smiled wistfully, watching the two of them together. They were a family. Chase was a father, and a good one. He'd taken on this responsibility when he was so young. He didn't have a choice. She felt a wrench in her stomach. If she'd stayed, she would have been a part of this family. Timmy would have been hers to raise, too. She wondered if Chase thought she didn't want kids or cared only about her career. She remembered the hopes and dreams they shared. But life had a way of throwing curve balls, high balls, and low balls, despite all their plans. He took on this role and never complained. He loved this child who reminded him of his brother, with the same big, intense blue eyes, and of Darlene, from whom he inherited the sandy blond hair.

She remembered the boyishly handsome Chase from ten years ago and her quickening heartbeat each time she saw him. His shy, crooked smile melted her heart. She knew why he smiled like that.

Katie sighed as her thoughts turned to her suitcase, packed and ready to go. She'd left once before, never looking back. In the years since, she'd achieved everything she aimed for, and then some. She was ambitious, single-minded, and smart. She should be fulfilled, but it felt empty and bleak instead.

"Hey," someone shouted, snapping her out of her thoughts as the kid zipped by to catch up with his friends. She glanced up to see Chase gather Timmy's backpack and lunchbox. He pointed in her direction, and the child's upturned face sought hers, waving excitedly when their eyes met. She knew Chase remembered she wanted to see the boy before she left. They headed her way, walking to the car.

The shrill sound of a ringtone startled Katie. She knew who it was before she glanced at the phone. She'd assigned it to one person—the BFH. A heavy weight gripped her chest as she paled. She stared at the screen, the number flashing, dreading this call, knowing it was never pleasant. Her finger trembled, poised over the "answer call" button. She counted the rings... one, two, three... then stabbed the button with her fingertip.

She swallowed and spoke, putting on her neutral, professional voice. "Hello, this is Katie."

Joanne didn't bother with any pleasantries, barking, "Where the hell are you?"

"I'm still here. I told Sally to cancel my flight. Did you get my message?"

"I put a stop to it."

"You did... what?" Katie gasped.

"You need to get your butt on that plane. NOW."

"But... I have a family emergency! I can't."

"You can. And you will. Do. What. I. Say. When I say—"

"No!" Katie cut her off. She'd heard enough. The veins in her neck pulsed and hardened, engorged with blood. When she spoke, she was slow and deliberate, enunciating each word. "You will *never, ever*, speak to me this way again." She took a deep breath. "Do YOU hear me?"

"B-but..."

"And one more thing—don't you ever call me again. I QUIT." Katie hit the button, ending the call.

33

KATIE OPENED THE PASSENGER DOOR AND GOT OUT, inhaling the fresh air. She remembered what it was like in elementary school. She remembered Mrs. Bell's solid oak desk with papers neatly stacked on top, pencils and scissors in a cup holder next to a sturdy stapler and tape, along with some scattered crayons, art materials, and some miscellaneous stuff.

Her desk was in the first row. She sat up front, squinting her eyes to see the writing on the whiteboard. It was later, when she was tested at school, that she found out she needed glasses.

She remembered carving her initials into her wood desk, staking her place alongside many who had sat in the same chair. Those old, scratched desks were probably gone by now.

"Hi, Katie." A tug on her arm accompanied by a smile on Timmy's face brought her back to the present.

She bent and hugged him. "Hi, how was school today?"

"Good." Timmy shrugged, eager to get going.

Chase hesitated, glancing at Katie. "Everything okay with you?"

Her eyes darted toward Timmy. He was standing right there beside them. Maybe this wasn't a conversation they should be having right this moment. "Yeah, it is now." Her lips curved slightly.

Maybe Chase misread her. He glanced away, pausing for a moment before he spoke. "I thought maybe something was going on. If... if there's anything I can do to help..."

She softened her voice. "Thank you. I can tell you this much: I won't be on the plane today. I've taken charge of my life and quit my job."

He sucked in a quick breath. "You're sure that's what you want to do?"

"I'm one hundred percent sure. I've thought about it long and hard, but I didn't have the courage to do it —until now."

He nodded and turned to open the rear car door, tossing the backpack and lunch box on the back seat. Timmy climbed in and buckled up. "Can we get some paint and drawing paper?"

"You got an art project?" Chase asked.

"Yeah."

"We'll get you something at the store." He waited for Katie to get seated, and when they were all buckled in, he cranked the engine.

He didn't have far to drive before she saw a store, Wally World—a smaller knockoff of the one in the big cities.

Timmy was the first one out, making a beeline for the store's art supplies section.

"He likes to choose it himself," Chase explained. "Knows what he wants."

She lifted her eyebrow, picking up her pace.

Timmy checked out the paint colors in the kids' section, picked out a washable paint set with eighteen colors, and handed it to Chase.

"That's what you want?"

He nodded.

Chase held the box up close to read the fine print. "It says nontoxic and washable," he said, patting Timmy on the shoulder. "Good choice."

Timmy put his hand up for a high five and grabbed a paintbrush set from the shelf. "I'll need these, too."

Katie had wandered down the aisle to check out the drawing pads for kids. She held up the three different sizes available—6"x 9", 9"x12", and 16"x22". "Which one?"

Timmy looked and pointed to the midsized pad.

"Okay, nine by twelve it is," she said.

"All set, Timmy?" Chase asked, balancing the items in his hand.

"Yup."

Chase paid, but before they headed out toward the car, he pulled out his phone and checked the time.

"We've got about another hour before we need to head back to the hospital. Let's drop these off at the house first."

34

Chase hadn't planned on taking Katie to his house. Seeing her today wasn't planned, either. He'd obsessed about it ever since Mary let the detail slip last night that Katie was leaving. He was hurt, too. She hadn't bothered to mention it. Had she planned on sneaking away, then?

He'd seen her talking on her phone while he was walking back with Timmy. She'd looked pale, shaky. He'd offered to help, but she didn't want his help. Maybe she didn't want it because she didn't want to be beholden to him or wanted to prove her independence. Whatever the reason, someone or something had shaken her up. He knew her. Instinctively, he had felt protective. But she took care of it herself. She was bull-headed that way.

He also had something he hadn't told her. In a few minutes, she would find out—when she saw his house and when she realized where he'd built it and why.

KATIE SNUCK a glance at Chase's profile as he was driving. If he knew she was watching, he gave no sign, just concentrating on the road.

He had said it was a short drive to the elementary school from his house. She knew this area well. It was on the outskirts of town. She rested her head and looked out the window at the rolling hills, green fields, and sparse houses on large plots of land with plenty of room. It hadn't changed much. She remembered how pretty it was here and how peaceful.

The car slowed down around the curve. Then she saw a flash of color and recognized Chase's red truck as he swung into the driveway.

"Wait... whose home is this?" She gawked at the stunning new house at the end of the driveway.

He grinned. "Don't you know?"

She knew this place when it was a field. She remembered how it looked with tall grass and beautiful wildflowers. She remembered how they laughed, ran, and romped in the field. She remembered telling him it was God's country, a piece of heaven on Earth, and she wished it could be theirs forever. She remembered he'd picked the most beautiful wildflowers for her and asked her to be his.

Her chin quivered, and her eyes welled with happy tears. She whispered, "I know," as she hugged him tight and kissed him tenderly with all her heart.

35

They went back to the hospital, leaving Timmy at home with the sitter. Katie called her sister while Chase drove.

"Hi, Mary, we're on our way. Where are you and Jim?"

"We just got here. Hold on a moment," she said, as an announcement over the speaker interrupted their conversation. "We're walking in."

"Can you find out if Momma is out of surgery?"

"Yeah, hang on while I check at the desk."

She heard muffled speech as Mary talked with the hospital staff, holding on to her phone. Chase turned into the hospital parking lot and maneuvered into a space.

"She's checking on Momma's status," Katie said, turning to snap free her seat belt as soon as he parked.

He locked the car and walked around to her side.

"Let's go," he said, his left hand reaching out to grasp her right one.

Her cheeks flushed. She was suddenly aware of his closeness and of the tingle at his touch when their fingertips brushed lightly. She slid her slender fingers between his until they interlocked. Her eyes met his and held them.

She dismissed the crackle on the phone and then realized it was Mary on the line.

"I'm sorry. Can you repeat that?"

"She's in the recovery room. When you walk into the lobby, go to the elevator. We'll wait for you guys there."

She ended the call and smiled at Chase. "They're meeting us by the elevator. She's out of surgery."

"Good."

They quickened their steps and followed the sign, meeting up with Mary and Jim. Someone had pressed the elevator button, and a ding announced its arrival. It was a tight squeeze to fit in all the passengers after a patient in a wheelchair was wheeled in.

When the elevator stopped at their floor, they got off. The nurses' station was down the brightly lit hallway. One nurse was on the phone, another nurse entering a patient's room, two others looking at notes on clipboards and conferring.

Chase caught the attention of a nurse sitting before a computer monitor.

"Can we see Mrs. Simmons?"

The nurse located her patient chart, flipping the

pages. "She's not awake yet. Once the anesthesia wears off, she'll be able to talk to you."

"How is she?" Mary asked.

The nurse glanced at the clipboard. "Dr. Fallon would be able to give you that information. I think he's still around here checking in with patients."

"The family is here now, and we'd like to talk to him," Chase said. "Can you tell him please?"

"I'll let him know."

"Thank you."

"Will she stay here?" Katie asked.

"No. She'll be moved to a private room." The nurse broke off, catching sight of Dr. Fallon and calling his name as he approached the nurses' station. He turned and saw Katie and Chase, his brows lifting in recognition.

"Doctor, I'd like to introduce you to my sister, Mary," Katie said, walking toward him and gesturing, "and this is her friend, Jim."

"Pleased to meet you."

"Do you have a moment to talk with us about our mother?" Mary asked.

"Yes, the surgery went well. She'll be experiencing pain after the anesthesia wears off. And there'll be some swelling. We'll be monitoring her condition here. When she goes home, she's going to need someone there to help her."

"Will she need to stay in bed?" Mary asked.

"No, it's better to be active. The therapist will show her some exercises to do."

"How long will it take for her to recover?"

"Each person is different. Your mother could take months or longer at her age. But proper care, a healthy diet, and exercise will help her recovery."

"Thank you, Dr. Fallon," both sisters said at the same time.

"The nurse will give her post-op care instructions and the number to call if she has questions. Be sure to do the follow-up appointments."

"We will," Mary said. "Thank you."

After the doctor left, a timer beeped on Mary's phone. She stared at it, covering her mouth with her hand and turning to Katie. "Oh no. I almost forgot. I need to take you to the airport now."

"It's okay."

"But you'll miss your flight."

"I won't be taking the flight."

"You're... not?"

"No, I'm not leaving."

"But... what about your job?"

"I quit."

Katie heard Jim gasp as Mary took a step back.

"The job was killing me, but I've cut out the cancer."

36

THE DAY MOMMA WAS RELEASED FROM THE HOSPITAL was a big deal. Katie, Mary, and Timmy made a ginormous "Thank You" card for the staff. Timmy personalized the card with drawings and colorful paints. Turned out, the kid had real talent. Everyone thought he did a great job, and the nurses couldn't stop admiring it and fussing over him. Chase was there, too, helping to get Momma in the car and driving her home.

They told Momma it was important to keep moving. She was going to rely on her walker during recovery—it could take several months for her hip to heal. She would need help with her daily activities, including getting dressed, cooking, bathing, and going to the bathroom.

Katie had moved back into her room, staying with Momma to help her. She'd turned in her resignation, in writing, the day she quit. She'd swapped the hectic, cutthroat life in the big city for the slow-paced, idyllic life in her hometown.

She settled into a new routine. She started cooking more, too, using healthy, fresh foods. Usually, dinner was set for a table of three for her, Momma, and Mary. On Sundays, Jim, Chase, and Timmy joined them for supper, and it was a full table of six.

Katie had hired someone to assist Momma on Friday nights, and as needed during the week when she had to run errands or take care of business. Momma was gradually getting better, but it was a slow process. She was determined to keep doing what the doctors ordered and stay active.

Friday night was date night—Katie's night off. Often, it was just her and Chase, but some nights, Mary and Jim joined them. They'd all see a movie and go out to dinner afterward. It was a lot of fun. They cracked jokes, and Jim's playacting of scenes from the movies they'd just seen brought on fits of uncontrollable laughter. He was a good sport, and he had a deadpan face perfect for his comedic acting. And it was on one of these nights when they were sitting at the diner, in-between the silliness, that things got serious.

It was Mary who started it by asking Katie what her plans were after Momma recovered well enough to be on her own. Was she going to stay in town? She had blushed, being put on the spot. But her sister had meant well, and Katie had been pondering this. Ideas had been swirling in her mind. It was time to put it out there, among family and friends.

"You're right," she said. "I've been thinking about this."

Katie reached for a clean napkin and dug up a black ink pen from her purse.

She scribbled on the napkin. "Here are a few ideas running through my mind," she said, and passed it around.

"You want to start a business. These are the ones you're considering?" Chase asked, scrutinizing the words.

"Yes, my initial thoughts, but I'd welcome input and suggestions."

Mary picked up the napkin. "So, I see cookie store, coffee shop, jewelry store, and craft shop. The first three are clear, but what's your thinking about the craft shop?"

"I envisioned this place with three parts. One part is a specialty store selling merchandise and cool items that other stores aren't carrying. Maybe I could start with just art sundries, special art items, coloring books, craft kits, scrapbooking supplies, stickers, et cetera. You get the idea. The second part is teaching, so we could have a classroom. If we need specific supplies for a class, the store can order it. The last part is to showcase talented artists of all ages, whether they are children or adults, even seniors." She sat back and glanced around the table. "What do you think?"

"I like it. It'd be an asset to the community," Chase said.

"I can't see you in the cookie shop." Mary frowned.

"What about the coffee shop?" Katie followed up.

"That's a possibility. But we have several dining options that serve coffee. Would there be a need for just coffee?" Mary paused. "Would you be considering a franchise?"

She shook her head. "No, I don't want to do that."

"How about combining the jewelry store and the craft shop?" Jim asked.

"That's an interesting suggestion," Katie said. "I can start small at first, and expand later. I'd have to draft up a business plan and run numbers on the costs. Thanks, guys, you've been really helpful."

Chase cleared his throat. "What about a name?"

Katie leaned back in her chair as a smile lit across her face. "It'll be Timmy's Place."

EPILOGUE

MOMMA GRADUATED FROM A WALKER TO A CANE A FEW weeks after the surgery. It still hurt all the time, but she never complained. She kept fighting and getting stronger every day.

Something else came back as her physical body healed—her spirit. Maybe having Katie back helped. Maybe having both her children there, surrounded by love, helped. Maybe it was time she got her life back. She knew Mr. Simmons would have approved. Maybe he was smiling from heaven now. One day she'd be joining him, but that was for another day.

KATIE AND CHASE got married on New Year's Day in the new home Chase had built on the exact spot where he'd first proposed to her.

Timmy was the ring bearer, carrying the couple's

rings down the aisle, resting on the small pillow made by the bride's mother, nestled inside a beautiful cedarwood box the groom carved for the occasion. He looked so cute in his little suit. He made a dashing figure, dressed in a white starched shirt and black suspender pants, with a bowtie and white flower boutonnière.

Momma was determined to give the bride away, and she did, walking with the assistance of her cane. Mary and Laurie served as the two maids of honor in the wedding. Katie wanted both of the women, and they shared the honor, walking down the aisle together. Jim was the best man.

They were married by Pastor Miller. His wife was the young Sunday school teacher who had taught a clumsy, shy Chase dance steps for his prom ten years ago. Her love and passion for music transformed this gawky teenager who'd asked for her help and put his trust in her. Her eyes teared as the pastor pronounced the happy couple man and wife, and they turned to face their new life together.

BOOKS BY JANE SUEN

Children of the Future

ROMANCE

This Time Around

EVE SAWYER MYSTERIES

Murder Creek

Murder at Lolly Beach

Murder off Route 82

FLOWERS IN DECEMBER TRILOGY

Flowers in December

Coming Home

Second Chance

ALTERATIONS TRILOGY

Alterations

Game Changer

Primal Will

SHORT STORIES

Beginnings and Endings: A Selection of Short Stories

ABOUT THE AUTHOR

Jane Suen is a *USA Today* Bestselling Author who writes mysteries, sci-fi thrillers, short stories, contemporary romance, and crime fiction.

Made in the USA
Monee, IL
31 July 2023